Sinner's Vow - Paperback

Murphy's Mafia Made Men

Vi Carter

CARTER BOOKS

Contents

NEWSLETTER

JOIN MY NEWSLETTER AND NEVER MISS A NEW RELEASE OR GIVEAWAY.

HERE

BLURB

Aidan

Following the death of our father, my brothers and I find ourselves on uneven ground.

We are reduced to nothing more than puppets controlled by our uncle Frank, the new leader of the South Irish Mafia.

In order to reinstate our foothold in the Irish Mafia, I agree to an arranged marriage.

I will stop at nothing to retain the title that belongs to us.

But the moment I lay eyes on Raven Collins, I know that she is dangerous.

So dangerous that I keep my distance.

That is, until she seeks me out, demanding my attention.

The closer she gets to me, the higher the body count grows.

Until all her secrets are exposed, and I vow to protect her no matter the cost.

Even if we are left standing in the ashes of the Irish Mafia.

Raven

Six months of marriage to Aidan Murphy, I'll win my freedom.

Not just mine, but my sister's, too.

This isn't my first marriage-- the first was to the Bratva, and I barely survived.

Now, my father has handed me to the Irish Mafia.

Aidan Murphy is a lethal man, one who owns me.

And the one who will kill me once he learns why I've been sent to him.

I need to stay focused and get what I came here for.

Before Aidan discovers the truth behind my lies.

Once I do, I win our freedom.

In order to do what my father demands, I have to get close to Aidan.

But the closer I get to him, the more I realize that betraying Aidan will cost me my heart.

Freedom comes with a heavy price tag. One I'm not sure we can afford...

ALSO BY THE AUTHOR

MURPHY'S MAFIA MADE MEN

SINNER'S VOW #1

SAVAGE MARRIAGE #2

THE BOYNE CLUB

DARK #1

DARKER #2

DARKEST #3

PITCH BLACK #4

THE OBSESSED DUET

A DEADLY OBSESSION #1

A CRUEL CONFESSION #2

THE CELLS OF KALASHOV

THE SIXTH (NOVELLA)

THE COLLECTOR #1

THE HANDLER #2

THE YOUNG IRISH REBELS

MAFIA PRINCE #1

MAFIA KING #2

MAFIA GAMES #3

MAFIA BOSS #4

BROKEN PEOPLE DUET

DECEIVE ME #1

SAVE ME #2

CHAPTER ONE

RAVEN

Dread drips down my spine in a slow trickle—my stomach clenches. On either side of me, doors line a long, daunting passage. Intentionally, I'm sure.

I'm positive my father revels in intimidating visitors as they shuffle toward his study at the back of the house, the ticking of the grandfather clock taunting them with each step.

The ticking that haunts me now.

For each hand movement accompanied by a tick, I'm another step closer to my doom. Father never calls me to his office for anything good. The last time he called on me, I ended up in the hands of the Bratva.

Raven, you can do this, I remind myself as I place one Jimmy-Choo-clad foot in front of the other.

A half-strangled laugh echoes back to me, and I press my lips together. Even as my fight-or-flight response kicks in, I keep moving forward.

Because, just like all the times before, I know I have no other choice.

You could run.

I shiver and grip the sides of my dress. The memory burns in my mind of what happened the last time I ran, not from my father but from my ex-husband.

I had run home to my father, pleading with him to save me from the beast of a man he'd given me to. It had been a risk, but I didn't know who else to run to. He'd put me in that situation, and I knew there was no escape unless my father granted it.

That day, my father held me as I cried bitter tears on the shoulder of his navy jacket. My sobs jolted my body, and I didn't notice him withdraw his phone, dial my husband's number, and tell my husband to come and collect his wife.

Knock, knock, knock. I've reached the dark wooden door that leads into my father's lair.

"Come in." My father isn't a man you ever keep waiting. My fingers sprawl across the door that I push open, and I step into his office. Olbas Oil tickles my senses. The white cloth handkerchief at my father's elbow is where the strong smell emanates from. My earlier breakfast curdles in my gut.

Three large chandeliers cast light down on the crown of his head. He shuffles paperwork on his mahogany desk. As my gaze travels across the bookcases that soar above my father, I find my calm by looking at a paper dove that Louise had made for him years ago. I have no idea why he kept the present from Louise, but right now, it's what I'm seeking—a moment of calm before the impending storm. I hope this time I'm strong enough to withstand the force of whatever he unleashes on me.

"Raven—"

I pull my gaze from the bookshelves and look his way. Maintaining eye contact isn't easy. His blue eyes always appear clouded, as if there's a madness lurking.

I keep my hands firm at my side, though I want to ball my fingers into fists so I don't fidget.

He gestures toward the adjacent chair. I descend into the brown leather seat before folding my hands onto my lap, waiting for the blow from his words.

He doesn't so much as blink as he leans forward and steeples his fingers on the desk. "You've won your freedom."

I release the breath I've been holding, and without being able to stop myself, I slump into the chair. My lips drag down, and my vision wavers. It's over.

Tears spill, and I'm smiling. I'm smiling with a fierce pain in my heart. God, the price I paid for my freedom had been branded into my flesh, literally. My ex-husband used his belt as his form of punishment.

"Thank you," I find myself saying through quivering lips. I'm crashing from exhaustion. I'm crashing from being relieved from an overwhelming crushing feeling. I'm free.

Free.

"Once you marry Aidan Murphy, you are free to leave this home. You can start over wherever you want."

I'm staring at the gray-peppered crown of my father's head, my vision as clear as a cloudless hot summer's day. His black fountain pen glides with fluid motions across a piece of paper.

"Excuse me?" My voice comes out strangled, pained, heartbroken.

Without flinching, he repeats his words as he continues to write. He pauses when I don't respond and glances up at me. "I need you to retrieve information from Aidan Murphy. Once you do, you have won your and Louise's freedom."

A whimper spills from my lips. The last time I extracted information from Victor, my first husband, it almost cost me my life.

"You said the last time that if I got you the information, we would be debt free." I'm speaking out of turn. I know I've crossed an invisible line even before my father looks up at me with fire in his eyes. His fist comes down with a heavy thud on the table, and I grip the arm of the chair so I don't jump.

"It helped," he grits out. "But it wasn't enough. Yes, you did well. You kept a roof over Louise's head. You say you want to give your sister a better life, but do you mean it?"

Louise. My Achilles' heel.

The information I obtained for my father gave him millions. Where did all that money go? I want to accuse him of returning to gambling, but I also value my life.

"Once you get the information from Aidan Murphy, you can leave him. Finances will be set up for you and Louise. I'd suggest you pull yourself together. Aidan Murphy may one day rule the Irish Mafia. He won't want a weak woman at his side." He returns to his work, dismissing me.

I'm so beat down that I don't at first comprehend the dismissal. When his gaze darts to mine, my brain stalls, mentally repeating his words before I rise. He has taken everything from me. I'm ready to walk away, but I can't. Not this time. I raise my head in defiance.

"No." My pulse builds to a tempo that's more fitting to a dramatic ballad grand finale. The part where the heroine dies, or the moment the hero realizes he's already lost her.

My father rises in one swift motion. He's a large man, over six feet tall, with massive hands.

"I wasn't asking, Raven."

"I don't understand." I blink tears.

His lips curl into a snarl. "You're a woman. You aren't meant to understand the ways of a man. Just get the information from Aidan Murphy, and you have your freedom." My father settles back into his chair.

"Or maybe he would prefer someone younger." My father's mouth curves into a smile. "Louise is very striking."

My stomach roils. His words should terrify me; instead, they make me want to tear the world apart. "You will not go near Louise."

My father ascends and steps around his desk with a raised hand. I fear what will come next. I've pushed too far, and I will pay the price.

The impact of the slap doesn't just burn my jaw; the force sends me sprawling to the floor. The ridges of the wooden floor dig into my palms. My hip takes the brunt of my fall.

I'm staring at the dark wood, panting and shaking. I want to get up. I want to defy him. Maybe he senses the rebellious nature in me. His fingers plunge into my hair, and my scalp burns as he forces my head back.

"Apologize."

I want to say no again, but as his gaze fills with brutality, I know this will end with me injured and still shipped away to marry a stranger. But, for one moment, it's brief. My defiance feels so good.

"No." My heart palpitates as I try to crawl away from my father before he can unleash his wrath upon me. The abrupt opening of his study door stops his assault.

My face continues to burn from the slap he planted on my cheek. I take in shiny black shoes before traveling my gaze up black slacks all the way to George's green eyes. My bodyguard isn't looking at me. A muscle tics in his square jaw.

George captures my father's attention. "I do apologize, Mr. Collins." He glances at his wristwatch. "I'm here to collect Miss Raven. The car is waiting."

My lungs constrict painfully. No one walks into my father's office unannounced, and George follows the rules. So why did he enter without knocking? Or did he knock, and I just didn't hear the sound?

I push off the floor. My arms tremble as if I'd been lifting weights.

"Get up," my father barks as he returns to his seat behind his desk. I hate him. I hate him so much. As I stand, my tongue flicks out, licking the blood off my lips.

When I'm upright, my father pins me with a stare. "The car can wait. Have one of the servants clean her up first," he says to George without taking his beady eyes off me.

My heartbeat thump, thump, thumps. George said the car is waiting. Am I leaving right now?

"Miss Raven." George's brash words have me pivoting toward him.

"I hope you show Mr. Murphy more respect. I'm sure his hand would be far heavier than mine."

I hunch my shoulders at my father's words. I want to rebel. I want to tell him I hate him, but I place one foot in front of the other until I pass George. The office door closes as George falls into step behind me. We walk down the long corridor, and I wrap my arms around my waist to try to shake off the growing fear.

"You shouldn't antagonize him," George whispers.

I take a peek at the forty-year-old man who has never spoken to me. I wonder how long he had been standing outside my father's office door. Responding would be pointless. George steps in front of me as we enter the ornate foyer of the house. We walk past the enormous staircase to the first floor, where I sleep. I'm looking around for my sister. I want to check on her, but no one is in sight to even ask about her.

When we reach my bedroom, George opens the door but doesn't enter. No one is permitted into our sleeping quarters. I had a hand in designing my room. The gold leaf that adorns all the matching white French furniture pulls the room together. It's a mix of contemporary and old world. The large black chandelier over my bed sends light dancing across the gray silk duvet. I find my gaze ping-ponging around the luxurious space. It's my haven, where I seek solitude on the hard days. I often thrash out my pain in my quarters and try to heal myself by decorating the space. I won't return here. I shake off the sense of loss and walk to my open closet.

I need to pack. My stomach squirms in pain, and I scramble for my calm, which in this moment, I can't find. I'm leaving again to marry yet another man. Will he hurt me as Victor had? A part of me wants to curl up and find a corner to hide in. I want to bury my head and let the time pass.

But gathering some possessions and saying goodbye to Louise spurs me to my walk-in wardrobe. I freeze as George greets my father on the landing. My dread grows as I spin around, fearing he's come to finish what he started in his office.

My father barges into my room and slams my bedroom door behind him. When he spins the lock, I know it's to keep George from interfering with whatever is about to come next.

I won't have anyone to save me this time.

CHAPTER TWO

RAVEN

I TAKE ONE STEP back, then two. I glance away from my father, praying for George to enter and make this stop. I'm staring at the locked door. I already know George won't enter. He can't. My gaze darts back to my father.

He smiles a smile that's been carved into his face by a rusty knife. "George won't come in. The door is locked."

I swallow as he advances toward me, and he doesn't stop until we stand mere toe to toe. The smell of Olbas Oil circles the air, and my stomach turns sour. My father towers over me, not just with his height but with his menacing aura, which curls my shoulders forward as if I can hide from him.

"I should beat you senseless for how you spoke to me in my study." His jaw clenches like he's bracing himself for the beating he wants to unleash on me.

My knees turn to sponges, and I lock my legs so I don't tumble to the floor. Fear chokes me.

He exhales, his warm, minty breath heavy on my cheek before his hand collides with it. The metallic taste floods my mouth, and I swallow the blood.

Hair covers my face, and I push the strands aside and look at my father. He clenches his fists, still not ready to stop. He followed me up here to continue using me as a punching bag.

I want to straighten my spine and raise my chin, but that will only anger him further. I keep my gaze on the floor and try to make myself appear small and obedient.

I must appear weak enough for my father, as he doesn't try to hit me again. Instead, he starts to speak.

"The Murphys have a knack for acquiring cheap property and turning it into a very profitable venture." He places his hands in his pockets.

I try to calm my beating heart. Blood at a snail's pace returns to my legs, making them seem less heavy.

"Rumor has it they're on the hunt again, and I want you to find out what property they're going to buy and where."

"How? I mean, it could take me months to get close enough to Aidan for him trust me." And even then, how will he give up such information?

My father spins around. "I'm sure you can be persuasive when you want to be."

I shiver, and I can't hold my father's gaze. He means to use my body. I wrap my arms around my waist as if I can shake off the uncomfortable sensation. Hasn't my body been used enough? I want to say no, again, at the unfairness of this situation, but my burning face keeps me from opening my mouth.

"If I were in your shoes, I would start with his office. Compliment him on his business, and you can build up to when his next venture will be."

I can't.

"Please..." I beg.

My father returns and stops only half an inch from my face. "You have disobeyed me already. This is the last time I'm saying this. You will marry Aidan Murphy. You will get me the information I require. If you don't, then don't come back. I'll have to find someone to marry Louise."

My body reacts with an airbag effect—the air rips from my lungs, my brain scrambles, and I try to calm myself by closing my eyes.

"You have six months. I need the information by then, or we will lose our home. You lose your privileged life," he spits out. "You and your sister are an expensive commodity that is a drain on my finances."

No, your gambling problem drains our finances.

"Six months, Raven, then your time is up." My father walks away. I assume, taking my silence as my agreement.

"Try to hurry for Louise's sake."

My father's cold words make me sick. He always uses what hurts us the most against us. He's right. I won't let Louise be sold off like livestock. After he leaves, I stare at the half-open door.

I'm left stunned and try to steel my nerves. I can keep Louise safe. I ignore my wardrobe, not caring about clothes. Having time with my sister will give me some calm before I leave. At the loud footsteps, I spin, unable for much more, but it's my mother who enters my room. She marches across the wide space. Her manicured hand grips my cheeks as she turns my head from side to side. The smell of her moisturizer clings not just to her skin but even to her clothes. It's a smell that sticks with my mother no matter what she wears. I want to yank away from her touch, but I hold still. "What did you do?"

"I said no," I answer with honesty, and my vision wavers. I feel a sense of victory, yet overwhelming defeat.

Is that pride shining in her eyes? "You've always had a rebellious nature, my dear. But men like your father want to crush that nature." She releases her hold. "You need to let that streak go. You need to obey if you want to survive."

One tear spills. "Like you?" I question. She has always obeyed my father. In my nineteen years on this planet, I've never seen her stand up to him. Did I want to end up like her? No, I didn't. I won't be like her. Yes, I will get the information out of Aidan, and then I'll have my freedom. I will return and take Louise with me. I refuse to allow her to succumb to the same fate as me.

Bitterness fills my mouth as if I've just sucked on a lemon.

"I obeyed before." I yank up the sleeves of my dress, showing the tops of my arms. The scars that run deeper than just the surface are on display, and my mother curls away from me in disgust. "Look where that got me," I bite, not showing the same restraint as I do with my father.

Another flash of emotion peeks out from behind her blue eyes. The look disappears. "You didn't obey him. You ran."

I want to tell her I ran because he beat me, but the damage is already done. My mother won't stop my father from handing me to another man. When I fall silent and let my sleeves conceal my past, my mother seems satisfied. She leaves and enters my bathroom, then returns with a damp washcloth. She cleans my face without a word. I study her features, seeking a mother in the hardened shell of the person who stands before me.

"My marriage to your father was arranged."

Shock, confusion, and repulsion slam into me. "I didn't know that," I whisper. Why didn't she ever share that information with me before? My mind skips back to when I was taken to Victor's home. My mother wasn't here. She had been on vacation with her sister when my father sold me.

A sad smile dances on my mother's ruby-painted lips. A knock on the open door has both my mother and I looking at George.

"Miss Raven." He bows his head at my mother. "Miss Collins. The car is waiting for Raven."

I haven't even packed. Did it matter? I have nothing with any sentimental value. "I want to see my sister." I place my hands behind my back to hide the tremble.

My mother shakes her head. "You can't."

"Please. Just five minutes," I beg.

My mother glances away. "He said no." She doesn't have to tell me who said no; she's speaking about my father.

My mother does something so unexpected that I can't find it in me to respond. Her arms wrap around me, and she pulls me into her embrace. "I'm so sorry."

My vision blurs, but she pats my back before releasing me. She won't look at me. Folding her arms across her chest, she focuses on the wall.

I want to beg and plead to see Louise, but I won't. It will only make things worse. I straighten my shoulders and walk toward George. Once again, I notice how the staff has all disappeared. Do they remember the last time I returned home broken and beaten?

The black Range Rover parked outside the front door isn't one of our vehicles. My father favors limousines. George looms behind me, and, at my hesitation, he reaches out to the door handle but doesn't open the door. "Mr. Murphy sent the car to collect you."

I can't move.

"Your bags are packed and in the back," George informs me when I don't move. I want to ask by whom and when did they pack my luggage? How long had this been planned? None of the answers would change the outcome.

"I can't do this." I blink at the girl in the Range Rover window, and she blinks back. I don't recognize her anymore. The last time I climbed into a car, I was terrified. This time feels worse. Turning away from my reflection, I look up at George. "I can't do this."

I have never seen a man appear so torn. "Miss Collins..."

"George. Please." I don't know what I'm asking him for. To use my name or to save me. I'm suffocating as the Range Rover hums at my back. I look George in the eye.

He presses down on the handle and opens the back door.

I'm deflated. I didn't expect him to do anything, but I wished for just a moment that someone would help me stop my father from giving me to men like a prize at the end of a fair.

"Miss Collins seems to have forgotten something. We'll just be a moment," George tells the driver, who nods. George closes the back door and turns to me. "Come now, Raven," George whispers.

And I'm following his six-foot frame back into the house. What are we doing? I have so many questions. I glance over my shoulder at the open front door and to the black tinted windows of the Range Rover. I follow George through the kitchen and out into the back garden. The flower beds rise on either side of me, and I'm passing a tree that I often read under when the weather grants us a clear day.

"Where are we going?" I ask George, the anticipation almost killing me.

George doesn't slow down, and I'm half running to catch up with him.

We walk toward a hedge that encloses the back of the garden. What is he doing?

"George?" I question again, and the desperation that swirls in my veins coats my words.

He walks toward the hedge, and I think he's lost his mind until a portion he touches dissolves, and it's then I notice the gate.

"If you follow this path, it will take you down to the beach."

I peek through the passageway before glancing back at the house.

"Raven." George gets my attention. "If you're going to go, go now. They'll notice you missing."

My hands twist the fabric of my dress. "Why are you helping me?" I know I shouldn't question his help, but he's never helped me before.

George has been my bodyguard for as long as I can remember, and not once has he showed me any affection. But right now, he places his hand on my shoulder, and his gaze tightens around the corners.

"I should have never let you go the first time. It's eaten away at me ever since." Shame fills his features.

"Now I have a second chance." His fingers tighten on my shoulder before he lets me go.

"What about you?" I hate putting him in danger.

His lip tugs up. "I'll be fine."

"What about Louise?" I have one foot in the passageway and the other on the lawn. I can't leave without her.

"You'll have to come back for her. If you're going, go now." The urgency in George's voice sways me, and I lean more toward the hidden path.

"You will never get this chance again."

George's final words spring me into action. I reach up and touch his cheek. "Thank you."

He jerks out his chin at the passageway. "Go."

I do. Dropping my hand from his face, I turn to the passageway.

Glancing over my shoulder, I watch George disappear as he closes the gate. It's like another world behind the hedge line of our property. If I wasn't running for my life, I might enjoy the otherworldly feel from the tunnel. I take a few tentative steps, careful where I'm placing my footing.

The thin walkway becomes almost nonexistent, as the underbrush has almost closed in the small passageway. I pause, and my heart thumps at the raised voices. Hairs stand on my neck. Loud male voices have me freezing. Something slams against the gate, and a squeal rips from my lips. I cover my mouth with my hands, and on trembling legs, I move back to the gate.

"I don't know." George's muffled voice makes me shift closer.

A large man blocks a small gap along the side of the gate.

The cock of the gun has bile rising in my mouth.

"Tell me where she is."

I'm ready to give myself up. I can't bear the idea of George being hurt. A face appears in the crack of the gate.

"Got her."

At the gleeful voice, I turn and run. Branches whip my face; they grab at my clothes and try to keep me rooted to the spot. Fabric tears as I struggle against the overgrown tunnel. Hair covers my eyes as I pull and tug myself out of the boney fingers of the branches. Sheer panic has ripped the fabric of my sanity, and I'm wrestling with the wildflowers. I don't know if I'm going the right way anymore. Voices reach me, but I can't see them. I continue to struggle. When I fall onto soft grainy sand, I take in a lungful of salty air. The steel gate bounces shut behind me.

The waves break and white foam fluffs up before it's all lugged back into the depths of the sea. Pushing up on my feet, I start to run like I know where I'm going to go and what I'm going to do. Like I have a plan, not a senseless fear of being handed over to another Mafia man who will break me this time.

Tears blur my vision, and I veer closer to the sea. The water breaks across my feet, and I dance away and collide with a solid chest. Everything inside me reacts at once, and I'm crashing. I've been caught. Running again was all in vain.

CHAPTER THREE

AIDAN

My shoulder collides with the solid oak door that rattles from the impact. I won't survive this again.

"Get a locksmith," the hotel manager orders the staff who linger in the hallway. We don't have time for a locksmith, but I don't voice this. I reserve all my energy for breaking the door down. The hotel manager has already tried one of the spare keys, but somehow William has managed to snap the key into his side of the lock, preventing us from opening the door.

"William!" I roar my baby brother's name before I throw my full weight at the door, which doesn't budge. I can picture him hanging from the rafters, a rope around his neck, his legs dangling in midair. His favorite brown shoes would be the first thing I'd see, I'm sure of it.

Panic takes full flight, and I switch from using my shoulder to my foot. I put every ounce of force behind the kick, and the door creaks, succumbing to my assault. "William!" All my hammering on the door isn't enough.

I take one quick look at the hallway filled with staff and management. I pause for a split second, wondering what my father would do.

I remove my gun and remind myself that he isn't fucking here anymore. I remind myself that he opted out.

The staff gasp as I raise the gun, aim at the lock, and squeeze the trigger. The bang of the gun would raise the dead from their sleepy graves, and it pulls squeals from the scrambling staff. None of them would be accustomed to someone firing a gun.

I brace myself as my foot connects, the door shatters, the lock buckles, and I'm forcing my way inside the darkened room. William found our father hanging in his office only a month ago. That would destroy even the strongest of men.

Fear.

Gut-wrenching panic.

Guilt burns through my veins, and blood rushes painfully to my chest. Everything moves in tandem with my fear, then freezes as my gaze rests on William. He sits on the edge of the bed, rubbing his eyes. His chest rises and falls.

My gaze swipes across the room, and I pause when I spot his favorite brown shoes on the floor. *On the floor, Aidan,* I remind myself, taking in a lungful of stagnant air. Seeing the shoes gives me clarity that my brother is very much alive.

I glance back at William, who looks at me through one eye. "What the fuck is with all the noise? Was that a gunshot?" He returns to pressing the heel of his palm into his eye sockets as I try to fight for control. I lean against the far wall and take in my brother and his even breaths. He's alive. He's very much here in the land of the living. Slowly, his gaze travels to my hand, which still clutches the gun. He raises two brows before returning to rubbing his eyes.

The silk sheets drape over the edge of the mattress and pour onto the oak wooden floor. Heavy red velvet curtains darken the room. A small gap in the curtains casts light across the bed.

"The staff couldn't get into your room, so they rang me." My voice sounds tight as I put my weapon away. Movement at the door reminds me we aren't alone. I walk to the waiting staff, and some hang back, fear tightening their eyes.

"Give us a moment," I say to the braver ones who attempt to peek in. I close the shattered door to try to give myself and William some privacy.

I know why William handpicks this hotel out of the hundreds our family owns. This one had been our father's baby. William seems to have a love-hate relationship with this particular building. He's drawn to it, yet he destroys the memory of what our father created with his endless acts of debauchery.

"Jesus, did you have to smash in the door?" William asks, rising off the bed. "You shot the fucking door?" He snorts a laugh.

I make my way to the large curtains and pull them across the bay window, which overlooks the pristine lawns. The fountain roars into the sky, water pouring back into a pond that's home to a bevy of swans. "You wouldn't answer the door." I find some balance and expel my earlier fear of losing William.

"Fuck's sake, Aidan. Close the damn curtains."

I ignore William's complaints and grab a trash can that's stowed under the mahogany writing desk. I gather up all the small plastic bags that have been strewn across the top of the desk. Specks of cocaine showcase the lines that would have been laid out last night.

"This isn't what the hotels are for." I grit my teeth as I speak before dusting the remaining traces of cocaine away. I want to add, *especially not this hotel*, but I don't.

I gather foil and tablets and also dump them into the trash can. I pocket his credit card and some cash left on the nightstand. Once I clear off the drugs, I pull the plastic bag out of the trash can and tie a knot on the top.

William runs his hands through his long black hair. "Why do you always have to piss on my parade? I was having such fun with my friends."

"I don't see any of your so-called friends, William," I bark. They all come when the party is in full swing, but I never recall them hanging around when the good times have come to an end. Each time I find my brother after the party is over, he's always alone.

Raising his arm, he attempts to shield his eyes from the light. "You must have scared them off."

I want to slap the grin off his face, but I won't put my hands on my brothers. William's a fuckup, but I know why he's a mess.

Him finding our father dead did a number on him. William shouldn't have been there, and I hate that I couldn't protect him from the image that I'm sure has seared itself into his brain. On that day, seeing the horror on my brother's face broke my fucking heart. We've done and seen a lot of shit throughout our lives, but to find your old man swinging from a rafter because he wanted to opt the fuck out—that stays with you.

"Get dressed," I order as I scoop up his shirt and throw it at him. William catches his shirt and pulls it over his head.

When William found our father, he cried, even when I warned him to stop as I fought the tightness in my chest. He hasn't cried since. Instead, he buries his head in drink, drugs, and between women's legs.

It's been a month since we buried the old man. A month of agony and change, not just in our family's life but in the Mafia life too.

"You look like shit," I say, glancing around the room, and the longer I look, the more damage I see. I run my fingers over my beard. "Frank's going to be pissed." I try to push my earlier fear away.

William's nose scrunches up as he sniffs a glass that holds remnants of last night's drink. "Fuck Frank." He swallows down the contents.

I tolerate a lot with William, but disrespecting Frank won't fly. "Don't forget that this is his hotel. Even the designer shirt on your back belongs to him."

I have zero respect for Frank myself. I personally despise the man, but I won't allow William to do the same. Frank might turn a blind eye to my odd rebellious incidents, but he won't be so forgiving with William.

He has zero tolerance for our younger brothers.

William's fingers tighten around the glass, and the anger storms through his eyes before racing down his arm. His fingers tighten around the tumbler before pitching the glass against the wall. The glass shatters across the wooden floor. William isn't done, not even close. He flips over a small three-legged table beside him. One of the legs snaps on impact.

"Feel better?" I ask.

"Fuck you!" His anger escalates, and he thrashes about the room.

The door opens, and I clear the distance quickly. Holding my palm against the cool wood stops them from coming in. "We'll be done shortly." I close the broken door and don't move away from it as William destroys the room. "Get it out of your system. We have a meeting," I say as I keep my back to him.

His frantic breaths shake his body as he stops tearing the room apart. "I hate him, Aidan." Pain radiates in my brother's gaze. Pain that I refuse to acknowledge a moment longer.

"You sound whiny, William. I'm getting bored."

My teasing does the trick. He stands a bit straighter, his brows rising like he can't fucking believe I said that. I push harder.

"What are you, a man or a boy?" I spin and square up to him.

He rolls his shoulders.

"A man or a mouse?" I proceed.

He juts out his chest.

"Pull your fucking self together." I speak down to him as I step closer to my baby brother.

He jerks his chin up before he grins. "I still hate Frank."

He's reeling in his pain as he slaps his cheeks like he can wake himself up fully. "Let's do this." He shoulders past me and opens the hotel room door. I follow him into the hallway. The staff hover close to the door; none dare to enter.

"The room will need to be refurbished," I say, though I don't address anyone in particular. After a while, hotel staff all starts to look the same. I'm sure one of them will pass the word on to the manager.

William slaps his pockets. "Where are my car keys? I'm driving."

We leave the hotel, and I get out my car keys. "Good luck with that. You parked in a ditch." I unlock my Mercedes and slide in.

William frowns in confusion, like he has no idea what I'm talking about. He must have been out of his mind last night not to remember crashing his car. He takes a final glance around the parking lot before he gets into the passenger seat. The leather creaks under his weight. He opens my glove compartment and takes out a pair of sunglasses before slapping them on his face.

"Where is the meeting?" He asks while pressing the button to let his window down.

"Birdhill." I pivot so I can see out the back window before reversing. The hotel grows smaller in the rearview mirror as I drive away and onto the main road.

I glance at William. "You're going to have to gather yourself."

"I'm gathered," he responds, pulling his phone out of his pocket. There are several small cracks across the screen. "Motherfucker." He unlocks the device and scrolls through his notifications. "Six missed calls?" He pulls down the sunglasses to look at me over the rim. "Stalker."

I grip the steering wheel. He's acting like a little fucker. "I'm serious about gathering yourself, William. Matty isn't well, and you might have to do some of his jobs." Our father kept us sheltered from a lot of the Mafia world. Instead, he placed his sons in the more legit jobs. But now that Frank, our uncle, runs things, we have to get our hands dirty. We have to do things that make all our moral compasses spin.

William stuffs the phone into his pocket, pushing the glasses up the bridge of his nose to cover his eyes, to cover his pain, which I know will start to raise its ugly head. William doesn't ask me what's wrong with Matty. It's a topic he refuses to speak about.

William turns up the radio, and the music blares from the speakers as we race down the road toward an uncertain future. Matty has dad's condition. He sees the world in gray, with no color. After Mam left, nothing made my brother happy. Depression—what a fucking beast.

Sometimes I wish Matty would use a drink or even drugs as an outlet instead of his sorrowful expression I think we all want to thump. The irony is, he looks like Father, too. I glance at my brother. His foot rests on my beige leather seat as he bobs his head to rave music. I want to turn down the music, but that would involve a conversation.

***

The hotel sits on the outskirts of Birdhill. Recent renovations have kept the doors closed. Half of the building has limited access, and that's the side where I park. The constant gazes that follow our every step often grows exhausting. At least here, no one watches us. As I turn the engine off and kill the music, William doesn't move. The bass still rings in my ears.

"We're here." I nudge his leg. He sits up as he removes his sunglasses.

"Keep them on. You look like shit."

William does as I say, and we get out of the car. I pull open the emergency double doors and enter the pool area. The pool has been drained of water, and the small mosaic pieces have been chipped away for the new tiling to be laid. But that's not what gets my attention. It's the man tied to the chair in the center of the empty pool that gives me pause. Blood trickles down the side of his face, and he's glaring right at me.

CHAPTER FOUR

AIDAN

A LARGE THUD ERUPTS as William jumps into the empty pool. He saunters toward the man, whose chin rests on his chest. The man isn't alert yet. "I think this might be a present for me." William grins and pushes the glasses to the top of his head.

I ignore him as Frank and my brother Jason enter the pool room.

Frank's blue Armani suit and white shirt make him look the part—the boss of our clan, the leader of the South Irish Mafia. I take Frank's outstretched hand as he walks toward me with a smile filled with glee.

His handshake tightens, the action deliberate. So there is no mistaking who holds the power here. He wears his crown of thorns with pride. No one would dare pull it from his head, not without drawing blood first anyway.

"You shaved," I remark, hoping to distract myself from the exhaustion that pulls at my mind.

"Don't I look younger?" He removes his hand from mine.

I look away from Frank and instead focus on Jason. He taps his hand against the side of his leg. The signet ring on his fifth digit makes a repetitive audible sound. After Father killed himself, Jason, like the rest of us, was knocked off his pedestal. Jason remains a formidable force. He's done things that would make the devil run from him.

Jason and I wear matching black suits. We're similar in physique and height, but I have Father's dark eyes, whereas Jason has our mother's green ones. His gaze appears void of any kindness. Maybe the rest of us brothers look the same. We've had to step up to the line, show our strength, and in more instances than one, we obliviated the line from the face of the earth.

When we snuff a man's life out, we lose a piece of our souls. Maybe that's why Jason's eyes hold nothing. Tearing my attention from my brother, I cast a quick glance at the man tied to the chair. I'm waiting for Frank to explain. William picks up a hammer that's been discarded and smiles at the tool that will become a weapon.

Frank clears his throat.

"I'm sure you're wondering who the man is." Frank holds out an arm, indicating for me to walk closer to the edge. We stand like gods on the pool's edge as the man starts to wake up. He doesn't hold fear as most men would. He isn't a regular guy. His dark suit and hard eyes scream security at me.

"Can I kill him?" William chirps while smashing the hammer into his open palm.

"Get out of the pool," Jason demands of our brother, and I'm glad Jason has stepped in. I'm exhausted and want this meeting over so I can go home. I don't have anyone to go home to, but at least I can be alone. At least I don't have to pretend that I've got my shit together.

William drops the hammer, and it makes a heavy thud against the tiles. He climbs out, and once he's standing along the side of the pool, only then does Frank continue.

"This man stole from me today."

The man in question watches us; once again, I notice how he isn't afraid. I want Frank to get to the fucking point.

"Then let me hurt him," William pipes up. The distaste curls Frank's lips. I shift forward, hoping to block William from Frank's view. My movement distracts Frank for now, but it won't always work.

"Aidan will kill him," Frank instructs.

I glance at the man. His eyes widen at Frank's order, his brows drag down, and panic infiltrates his calm.

I don't want to kill anyone today, but I remove my jacket and roll up my sleeves. I jump down into the pool and extract my gun. Flesh and bones. Nothing more, I remind myself as I point my gun at his head.

"It must be long and painful, Aidan. We must send an example to people who steal from me. From us," Frank finishes.

I put my gun away.

"He stole something that can't be replaced. Lucky for you, George, we found Raven."

I have no idea who Raven is, but George fights his restraints. He doesn't shout profanities or threats; he struggles like he might break free. The hate in his eyes directed toward us makes me like him just not enough for me to disobey Frank's order and let him live.

"This is Aidan." Frank points at me. "Raven's future husband."

Husband? I glance at Frank, and his smile reminds me of a shark circling blood. "There is no easier time to tell you this, but you will marry Raven Collins."

That's one thing I refuse to do—enter into any kind of marriage. For the Mafia, an arranged marriage isn't unusual, but it's not for me. Everything I touch, I break. Women warm my bed, but I don't ever let the relationship go any further. My gut squirms with the thought of a wife. I'll kill for my uncle and make deals with the worst kind of people, but I won't do marriage.

Before I can tell him it isn't happening, he continues.

"She is the future." Frank steeples his fingers against his lips. He leans in as if we're sharing some unearthed secret. His smile fucking annoys me. "She is the future of the Murphys' expansion in the hotel business."

I steel myself before I glance at Jason, and he won't meet my gaze.

William snorts beside me, but I ignore him. "I need a drink," I say.

"You need to learn your place," Frank barks, unable to ignore William like I'm trying to.

I hold up a palm to let Frank know I can take care of it. Turning to William, I flash him a warning. "Go and get one, then."

Hatred—that's what I recognize in William's eyes. Disgust at my obedience to Frank. He has no idea of the pressure on my and Jason's shoulders to keep us in the position we find ourselves in. Frank could pull the rug out from under our feet if he pleased, and we wouldn't have a leg to stand on. We wouldn't have a roof over our heads or a pot to piss in. So placating him, for now, is the key to our future.

"None of this is right." William pushes past me, his anger propelling him from the room.

"You need to teach him some manners." Frank directs this to Jason. He doesn't give Jason a moment to respond and continues. "If I spoke to my elders like that, my father would have taken something from me." He holds up his hand that has only four fingers. We've heard this story too many times. "Like a finger," Frank finishes.

I want to ask him if I pinned William's hand to a table and sawed off his finger, would he shut the fuck up, but he isn't speaking to me.

"Aidan and I will have words with him, so leave it alone." Jason's deep, gravelly voice has a way of making men shiver. But not Frank. Frank doesn't retreat or shy away.

Kings don't bow.

Frank exhales like he's dealing with amateurs.

"I have spoken to Raven's father, and to expand both our businesses, you will marry her. Unite the families. This will be the culmination of everything."

I'm looking from Frank to Jason, and my gaze slides to George, who fiddles with his restraints. Some sick part of me hopes he escapes so I can hunt him down.

"No, marriage isn't for me. I'm sure Jason or even Alex..." I pause and look around the room for my older brother. "Speaking of Alex, where is he?"

Frank waggles his fingers. "You are not changing the subject. We voted, and you will marry Raven."

"Ah." I'm looking at Jason. That's why he's all uptight and not meeting my gaze. "You voted without me." My composure slips. "I have no say at all."

"As I said, we voted, and you will marry her." Frank's tolerance of us evaporates, and the man I'm used to seeing returns. The one who doesn't negotiate. The one who tells you what to do, and you do it. The one who would extinguish a life as if he were blowing out a candle.

"I'm too busy," Jason explains. I'm not sure if he notices my growing irritation, and that's why he explains to me why he can't marry Raven. My tie feels tight, my shirt feels tight, and the air in the room feels tight. I turn back to George, whose eyes widen.

"Your bride is already at your home. Unfortunately, she didn't arrive unscratched." Frank glances at his silver Rolex. "So, I suggest you hurry up."

My blood boils at the idea of Raven being marked. I didn't want her, but she is mine nonetheless, and the idea of someone hurting what I own makes me want to do some serious damage. I step closer to George.

"I'm her bodyguard." George speaks for the first time. "I tried to protect her."

I kneel down so we're eye level. "Protect her from me?" I point at myself.

His jaw clenches.

This man doesn't deserve to die. "I won't kill him," I say without looking at Frank.

"You will, Aidan. Your father left this company bankrupt, and I had to build it back up. I'm trying to make it stronger. So you will kill this man, and you will marry Raven."

I've always believed Frank, but right now, I feel like I'm being led down a dark path. I have no choice. There never seems to be one.

I stand up.

"If you do, we get ten percent," Jason speaks up, and everything starts to make sense.

"Ten percent of the company?" I ask. It's less than we're willing to take, so placating him, for now, is the key to our future. Only, our father was too weak. The thought of my father's weakness churns in my stomach.

"Ten percent of the profits." Frank widens his arms. The glint in his eyes tells me he knows how unreasonable that offer is.

"We want our names on the papers," I say and try to hold my voice steady.

He nods.

"I'll marry her." Agreeing doesn't mean I have to like this situation or spend time with her. If all this marriage takes is our names on paper, then I might be able to pull this off.

I should say more. I should do more. But do I have a choice? I have to marry her, but that doesn't mean I have to be in her presence. The longer I stare at George, the more I know this won't end well for her. Not with a man like me. Anger pumps with rapid fire through my blood, and I withdraw my gun. Without blinking, I release several rounds into George's chest.

CHAPTER FIVE

RAVEN

I WON'T CRY. I keep the mantra in my head as I'm manhandled and placed in the back of the Range Rover. The door closes, and it's too loud, too final. As the vehicle pulls away from the beach, I pivot so I can see the empty seaside. I'm searching, seeking out one person. As the sea fades into the horizon, I fear what may have happened to George.

"Where's George?" I push my messy hair out of my face, tempted to pick out the leaves and small twigs that have tangled themselves there, but I need an answer. I need to know he's okay.

I ask what I truly fear. "Did you hurt him?" The thoughts of George in pain have guilt pounding into my conscience.

"I never laid a finger on him." The nasally voice draws my focus to the passenger's gray eyes in the rearview mirror. He's the one who said "Got her" back at the gate. I turn away from him, conserving my energy, and I try to push my fear away. I examine my hands. Small cuts from the thorns have drawn blood. The wounds appear minor. I shouldn't have run. I shouldn't have gotten George involved.

I tell myself that he's at home, safe, and focus on thoughts of my sister. Six months and I can give her a better life.

The driver and the nasally sounding man take turns looking at me, and being stared at feels so foreign. I have been kept locked up at home for the last year, not seeing anyone, only our staff.

I sink back into the black leather upholstery and try to calm my racing heart. The last time I was shipped away, I had an odd notion of finding love in my new husband. I was seventeen at the time—so young, so naïve, so stupid.

My ex-husband, Victor, was fifteen years my senior. I was a toy he wanted to play with and break. A tear falls. He broke me, time and time again, and I've spent the last year trying to fix myself. But, I soon realized there was no fixing what he had done to me. He took my virginity violently, and that was only the start. How am I ever going to survive this all over again?

I am wiser, and I like to think stronger, too. Betty, our house manager, says I have an old soul. But she's wrong; it's not old. It's damaged.

My face aches, and I reach up, touching my cheek. Small specks of blood appear on the tips of my fingers. A ball of fire burns in the pit of my stomach, and I have this odd sense that I might explode as I stare at the stark red blood. I inhale a deep breath and let out a shaky puff of air. Glancing out the window, I take in the trees.

Trees, trees, and more trees give way to fields. The blue sky hangs low over the black cows in the far away fields. They graze and eat their fill, none the wiser that they'll go to slaughter. I have been groomed and trained, but I know I'm going to the slaughterhouse. My fingers inch closer to the handle of the door. I could open it, fling myself out and end this nightmare. What would Aidan do if he learned I tried to run? Victor relished every second of punishing me when my father returned me to him.

The image of my sister's face in my mind causes me to fold my hands in my lap. My fingers entwine, my nails dig into my hands, the pain keeps me focused and keeps me from reaching out and opening the car door.

The car begins to slow after a while and pulls up to a set of large wrought-iron gates. The security guard in the passenger seat speaks to someone through his earpiece. "We have Miss Collins with us."

The gates open painfully slow, and my heart palpitates. As we enter the grounds, I glance back to watch them close. Security cameras and men circle the fortress that we pull up to. The sun beats down on the gray stone mansion, but no matter how much sunshine there is, it can't remove the cold that emanates from the house. Ivy climbs along two of the prominent structures in the front of the building. We stop at the steps that rise up to the white double front doors that open, then what seems like an army of people emerges.

A gentleman dressed in all black approaches the rear hatch. A woman in a black tunic opens my car door. With a bow of her head, she greets me.

"Welcome, Miss Collins." She holds out her hand to help me out, appraising my marked face and arms. Once my feet touch solid ground, she releases me. I should try to straighten my attire, but I'm beyond salvaging my dress. Security men flank me. There's more security than I've ever seen. A butler waits at the double doors while two other servants carry in my suitcases. I'm escorted to a large drawing room.

"Master Murphy has been informed of your arrival. I'm Donald, Master Murphy's personal butler." Donald, who I'd guess is to be in his late fifties, speaks as he steps into the room. He gestures to a chaise lounge that I'm standing close to. My knees bend as I lower myself to the edge of the seat. I glance around the large, impressive room.

Donald gives me an odd look and clears his throat. One of the security men steps into the room. "She may need some attention." He speaks to Donald, like I'm not sitting here.

"I was given strict instructions from Frank to have her waiting for Master Murphy. So she shall wait."

Hairs rise along my arms.

There is an air of arrogance that coats Donald's words. The security man doesn't leave. "You want me to look bad?" He presses a black piece in his ear.

"You don't need my help," Donald mumbles as the security man turns away and speaks into a mic that's attached to the sleeve of his jacket.

Donald straightens his waistcoat and bristles. He reminds me of a peacock fluffing his feathers. "The front part of the pavilion mansion has undergone renovations," Donald says with pride in his voice. He steps up to a large fireplace. "This grand fireplace was rescued from a castle."

It's magnificent. I nod and reach for the cushion beside me. My fingers touch the gold tassels. I'm trying to ground myself.

Donald strides to one of the walls that's adorned with paintings. He points to a landscape image. "This painting is by the famous painter, William of Isles."

I've never heard of him. I wonder how many times Donald's made this speech. I wonder if it's his way of keeping the guests occupied whilst they wait. No matter what he tells me, it doesn't stop my mind from spinning.

Movement in the foyer has my brain freezing.

"Master Murphy," I hear on repeat from the staff. My pulse picks up to a crescendo I don't recognize, and I fear my heart will give out. I'm not ready. I'll never be ready for this moment. A man enters, and he dwarfs everything around him. I stand resolute and hold my breath as my future husband takes me in.

He approaches me, and I find myself recoiling from him. He doesn't pause. His footfalls echo against the wooden floor. His large hand touches my cheek, and I can't help when my body flinches, and the backs of my legs bump against the seat I had been sitting on. Eyes so dark roam across my face, and fear skitters down my spine.

"Donald." His deep voice sends a shiver skidding across my flesh. Looking away from me, Aidan continues to speak. "Ask Raven why she ran." His words dig into my flesh.

I feel like a trapped animal. Panic rises hard and fast, and I try to still my mind.

"Of course, Master Murphy." Donald's attention falls on me, his gaze prodding into mine, wanting me to answer. "Why did you run, Miss Collins?"

My voice is no longer where it should be. It's hidden deep down inside me. Aidan's large hand leaves my cheek, and my body grows slack.

He tilts his head.

And something propels the words from my lips. "I'm sorry." The lie falls with ease. I'm not sorry. I'm sorry I got caught. But, I'm not sorry I ran. I lower my chin, which has risen as the rebellious thoughts take center stage in my mind.

"Raven."

Fear curls in my stomach at how he says my name.

The bow of lips curls into a snarl, and he takes a step closer to me. I feel smaller than a child being scolded. My body stings, and it feels like the flesh on my bones tightens. I inhale the scent of his cologne and a bite of coldness.

"You aren't sorry."

My fingers tighten together, and I try to reel in my panic. I give a quick shake of my head. "I am," I admit as the reality of what I have done starts to sink in—my vision wavers.

Aidan's brow rises, and I wait for him to react, but his stoic expression sends tremors through me.

He gives a curt nod of his head and turns away. "Show her to her room." Aidan's broad back faces me as he leaves the room.

My legs threaten to give out, but Donald holds out his arm. "Miss Collins. This way."

My mouth moves without my permission. "Is George okay?" I ask the question I shouldn't ask.

Aidan's footfalls stop, and when he glances at me over his shoulder, I want to grab the words and stuff them back into my mouth. His eyes darken, and I hate how every cell in my body expands to a bursting point as he walks back to me.

"No, he's not okay." He's snarling again.

I'm standing on a cliff, and I'm ready to jump. I can feel the pull of the ocean below. There's no way out of this, only down.

"You are the reason he's dead. Your privileged little world drags men like George to their graves." His gaze grows distant. "Did you promise him something in return?"

He steps even closer; his breath brushes the bridge of my nose. I'm dizzy with fear.

"Pretty little girls like you are only good for one thing."

My lungs feel painfully constrained. I'm tempted to look up into Aidan's face, but the malice and violence that's vibrating from him keeps my gaze downcast. My hands tighten around the fabric of my dress.

A whoosh of air accompanied with a sneer dances across my cheeks. "I want to know what you promised him."

"Nothing," I whisper as I battle a tsunami of tears. George is dead. Did they torture him?

"Get her out of my sight." Aidan steps away from me, and once again, I'm ready to crumble, but Donald waits with an outstretched arm, just like he had before.

I follow him numbly, and two security men fall into step behind us, along with two female servants. Our entourage follows us in silence up an imperial staircase. We stop at the first landing, and I'm shown to my quarters. The security settles themselves on either side of the door. Donald doesn't enter, but the two females do. The butler arrives with my luggage, and I stand frozen as he places my suitcases on the queen-sized four-poster bed. One of the females yanks down the zippers of my bags and starts to remove my clothes. My hands itch to stop her. I don't like anyone touching my possessions, my tie to my former life, but I stand still and watch as they empty my suitcases and put away my clothes.

I'm waiting for the repercussions of me running away. *Was George's death not enough of a punishment?* I want to scream.

Once I get the information my father wants, this charade will end.

That's the mantra that keeps me still as the realization that this is it sinks in. Only hours ago, I had been in my garden reading a book, and now here I am, soon to give my body to another man. Only this time, I'm not going in with any illusions of love. I will protect my heart, no matter the cost. But my body and mind? That's an entirely different matter.

CHAPTER SIX

AIDAN

THE INUNDATION OF VIOLENCE in my body has my fists tightening. I walk away from Raven and make my way to my office, which is situated at the rear of the pavilion mansion. This place has been in our family for generations. It's the last piece of our legacy I haven't been able to let go of. I fight the urge not to make the call, not to ring her father and threaten him for being so incompetent. He had one simple job and that was to place Raven in a car that Frank had arranged for her. Yet she managed to escape, hurt herself, and get her bodyguard killed in the process.

I exhale a slow breath before sinking back into my seat. My mood plummets each time I think of the meeting and Frank's meager offer of ten percent. He and my father split the company fifty-fifty. When my father died, he had nothing in place, so one hundred percent of the company went to Frank.

A knock on my office door causes me to straighten in my seat. Automatically, I stack papers together on my desk in an attempt to make my workspace look presentable.

My hands still as Jason enters. "You left abruptly after the meeting." He pushes the office door fully open. "I wanted to make sure you were okay."

"I'm great. On top of the fucking world." My lip quirks up. I wouldn't call killing someone a meeting. Frank hadn't been happy that I didn't give George a slow death, but the fact I agreed to marry Raven made him back down.

Jason isn't amused. He closes the door and walks along the row of bookshelves that hold all our father's books, ones I've never read and most likely never will.

Jason takes a brown file from under his arm and places it on my desk. I don't ask him what it is. Instead, I flip open the front page, and I nod before looking back up at Jason. "She's a beauty," I say as I grit my teeth. The images of Raven don't do her beauty justice.

I flip through all the photos, and one makes me pause. She's holding a snow-white bunny, the creature tucked securely to her chest. She won't last a second in our world. I peer up at Jason, who watches me carefully.

I try to quench the violence that continues to pulse and pour through my system. The fact they picked me completely baffles me.

Jason gives me a side-eyed glance. "Your wife."

Gripping the desk, I try to remain calm with my brother. "The woman you voted for me to marry."

His lip tugs up humorlessly. "You know the rules, Aidan."

Rules and more fucking rules. When we worked for my father, we helped run the hotels. He never let us peek behind the curtain that shielded us from the Mafia world. The foundations of our empire are drenched in so much blood. When I don't respond, Jason continues.

"She is your property. You can do with her as you wish." Jason's features turn impassive.

"So, I could kill her for trying to run?" I lean back in the chair, and the idea of killing her pulls a smile to my lips.

Jason fires me a warning look. "You can't kill her."

I wanted to. I wanted to end her life for trying to run. She had forced my hand already—she made me kill George. My fear of her pushing me again makes me close my mouth tightly. I need to let the idea of hurting her go. I pick up a pen and tighten my grip around it.

Seeing her standing in my drawing room earlier, with her messy hair and cuts and scratches, did something to me. The want to hurt her father for allowing this to happen became overwhelming. Her crystal blue eyes sparkled with fear, stealing all of my attention.

The danger of a woman like Raven lies in her beauty. I can't have her near me. Already, I want to hunt her father down and hurt him. She's bringing out the worst in me. She's lethal, and I can't have her around me much longer.

"Patrick and Gilly will be here at eight thirty."

I pinch the bridge of my nose as I sink into my chair. I exhale as if it might let some of the anger leak out of me. No matter how many times I try to purge the rage, it's like it empties but fills right back up. "I forgot about them." I lower my hand.

"I know, but Uncle Frank wanted me to give you the reminder."

My mind spins with words that I don't allow to surface. Has Jason stepped over to the dark side with Frank? I sound like William. I give a quick nod in acknowledgment of Jason's words. Gilly is Frank's son and our cousin. He doesn't have much involvement in the Mafia world, but I suspect Frank wants that to change. He wants him to start spending time with us.

"Alex and Matty won't be coming to the get-together." Jason digs his hands into his pockets.

I get why Matty isn't coming. I don't want him here. Guilt glides and dips along the base of my gut. "Alex has been very busy lately." My words sound resentful. I am. I am resentful of how much our eldest brother seems to get away with. He's always missing, and the workload lands on my and Jason's shoulders.

Jason finally sits down, and the conversation turns to the offer our uncle made and us only getting ten percent. It's a start. That's something we both agree on.

Gone are the days when we competed for who could close the largest deal the fastest or who could find a hotel that had been closed by default, and we bought the premises for pennies. It was a game for us. A game that we thought would never end.

Now, all we know is pain and violence. Restrictions and rules.

Once Jason leaves, I dig the palm of my hands into my eyes to try and relieve some of the stress, but it doesn't help. I leave my office and go in search of Donald to inform him of our arriving guests.

He's busy in the main living room. I pause at the foot of the door. "We have guests arriving soon," I say.

"Master Jason informed me."

I snort. Of course he did. I walk away to get ready for the party.

***

William rocks on his heels as he drinks from a long-neck bottle. His eyes dance with madness. "Are we going to get this party started or what?"

He puts the beer down on the mantelpiece. My hands itch to remove the bottle or grab a coaster. The 19th Century Château Solid Carved Oak Ingle was another restoration project I had shared with my father. I shift in my seat at William's blatant disrespect.

Patrick, my cousin's friend, takes out a plastic bag of powder. "Yes, we are." His shrill voice bounces around the room. I meet Jason's gaze as Patrick pours the cocaine onto the coffee table, and William joins him in taking a line.

"Aidan?" Patrick holds out a rolled-up note while wiping his nose. I watch the cocaine flood his system.

I raise my glass of brandy. "No, thanks."

He shrugs and offers the same to Jason, who declines. Gilly keeps glancing at Jason and me. He's not sure how to act. I take a sip of my drink, not offering to help him navigate the rough waters he's gotten himself into.

"No, thanks," Gilly says.

This is his first step. Frank did the same with us. He let us mingle with the men, then party. Women, drugs, and drinks came next. Debauchery all flowed and ebbed together until we had to make our first kill to become made men.

I empty my glass, burying the fresh memory. A month ago, we had to show we were men. A month ago, that changed us all.

William dips his head for a second line of cocaine, and Patrick gears up to do the same.

William stands and lets out a heavy whoosh of air before grinning. "So, where is your wife?" he asks, returning to the hearth and picking up his bottle of beer.

"Why?" I ask.

Jason stands and brings the bottle of brandy over to me, where he refills my glass. I'm sure I look like I need a drink. He fills it halfway before he sits back down. Gilly watches Jason's every move.

"Is she hot as fuck?"

My head whips to William. He's still grinning.

"You got married?" Gilly sits forward.

"I'm entering into an arranged marriage for the company's benefit," I educate him.

"What the fuck? In this day and age?" Patrick takes a cigarette out of its pack and lights it up. It's not something I normally permit in my home, but I take a sip of brandy to steady the irritation his presence causes me.

"What do you do, Patrick?"

He points at himself. "Me?"

"No, the fucking clown behind you." William sneers and takes the pack of cigarettes from Patrick's hand.

Patrick's smile grows unsteady. "My father owns garages. I work for him." He blows out smoke.

I nod. "We don't just run hotels. We hurt people who don't follow the rules that have been set in stone."

Patrick frowns and glances at Gilly.

"What my brother is saying is that an arranged marriage is normal to us," Jason, ever the diplomat, intervenes.

I savor the brandy and let William do the talking, which he enjoys. I watch him as he flicks the ashes into a crystal bowl, using it as an ashtray.

"I want to see her," William pipes up. "I just don't believe it."

Jason quirks a brow. I don't want Raven down here, but I know William won't shut up until he sees her.

"Is she ugly? Is that why you won't bring her in here? Does she have a hump on her back?"

I want to tell William to shut the fuck up.

William grins. "Are you afraid she might be won over by my charm?"

"I would like to meet her too." Gilly sits forward in his seat as he speaks, buying into William's demands. William opens his mouth to harp on.

I hold up a hand. "Fine, tell Donald to bring her down." I don't move from the chair, but the moment I give William permission to get her, I regret it.

CHAPTER SEVEN

AIDAN

WILLIAM EXTINGUISHES HIS CIGARETTE in the crystal bowl with force. He doesn't like to be told what to do, but his curiosity about seeing Raven wins out, and he leaves to tell Donald to get her.

I sense Jason watching me but refuse to look at him. Instead, I finish my drink. Gilly and Patrick laugh and chat, and when William returns, he gives me a raise of his bottle. "He's getting her now."

I glance at the sitting room door, where Donald stands, waiting for my confirmation. I give a nod of my head, and he leaves to get Raven.

My gut squirms with the anticipation of seeing her. Maybe it wasn't just for William. Maybe I like looking at her pretty face. I can look, but that's as far as this relationship will go.

"What garages does your father own?" Jason asks Patrick.

"Lexus, Ireland. We have fifty-three stores across France, Ireland, and the UK." Pride has Patrick standing taller.

I keep taking peeks at the door, waiting for Raven, and when she appears, I find myself sitting up straighter.

She places her hands behind her back as she steps into the room. Donald gives a bow as he steps outside the door. He doesn't leave; I don't intend to allow Raven to stay long.

"This is Raven Collins." I rise, leaving my glass of brandy on the small circular coffee table. She swallows as I walk closer to her. Her blue eyes grow wider and fill with fear. "My future wife."

Her lids flutter closed for a brief moment as if the words pain her. She hasn't moved from the door. The small cuts on her face have been cleaned, her hair washed and freshly brushed. The refreshing scent of honey wafts in the air.

"Let her in so I can take a look," William speaks up. His voice carries a light tone, but his words darken my mood.

Raven's mouth opens and closes, and I take a step back, letting her into the room.

"Take a seat." I point at one of the vacant couches. She walks with stiff shoulders to the couch and perches herself on the edge. I retake my own seat.

"Hi, Raven, I'm William, Aidan's better-looking brother. I'm sure you feel you got robbed with his mug."

William holds out his hand, and I grip the arm of the seat to keep myself from dragging William away from her. Raven takes a quick, frightened look at all of us before taking William's fingers. He, of course, takes it one step further and plants a kiss on the back of her hand.

"Nice to meet you," she says in a soft, small voice, and I'm ready to dismiss her, wanting her back safe in her room. I pick up my empty glass to give my hands something to do.

Raven chews on the inside of her cheek.

"This is Jason, my brother." I point at him with my glass of brandy. Jason appears almost uncomfortable with having Raven here. I hope her presence reminds him of how he threw me under the fucking bus.

"Gilly, my cousin." I point at Gilly, who gives Raven a nod of his head.

"And Patrick," I offer last. Patrick grins and sits down on the couch beside Raven.

"Where are you from?" William asks, oblivious to the growing tension in the room.

Once again, I find Raven glancing at me. When Jason rises again, he blocks me from seeing Raven as he fills up my glass. Once he's seated, I sip my drink and try to appear calm.

She's looking at William. "Newport, here in Tipperary."

"Ah, that's a cool area," Patrick chirps, and he's sitting a little too close for my liking.

Patrick continues on with a slew of questions for Raven. Each one, I listen to. He asks her age, which I discover is nineteen. She doesn't work, which isn't a surprise. She was homeschooled, and she has a sister, Louise. I sip my drink as Patrick continues to extract information from Raven that only belongs to me.

Gilly and William break off into their own conversation, no longer interested in Raven.

"I wanted to have a word about Matty," Jason says low enough so only I can hear. He snaps my attention away from Raven. My fingers tighten on the glass of brandy.

"What about him?" I ask before taking a drink like I can brace myself for what comes next.

"He's becoming more withdrawn."

"So, what? You want to do a brother intervention?" I sneer, hoping Jason will hear my resistance and let this subject go. Being around Matty is such a reminder of our father, and honestly, I can't bear it.

Jason taps his hand on the arm of the chair. The signet red ruby ring catches my attention—an heirloom from our grandfather that Jason has worn every day since Father's death. Another fucking reminder that I don't want. "Yes, I think we need to do something."

I empty my glass. "Like what?" I don't get to hear Jason's response. My attention zeros in on Patrick, who has moved closer to Raven. His fingers trail down her arm. It's like a red flag to a bull. Everything in me boils, and as Jason speaks, I hear his voice but not his words as I place the glass of brandy down on the table and stand.

I'm in control of each step as I walk over to Patrick and Raven. Raven's wide blue eyes take me in, but I focus on Patrick, whose face pales as I stand over him.

"Is her skin soft?" I ask.

Patrick's cheeks redden, and he looks to Gilly for help.

I click my fingers in his face so he focuses on me. "I asked you a fucking question."

"Yes, I suppose. It was just a touch," he tries to defend himself. He forces a shivery smile before shrugging. "It's no big deal." He half laughs.

Like a man possessed, I grab him by the scruff of his neck and drag him off the couch.

"What are you—" he starts as I toss him to the floor.

Before he can react, I bend and place my knee on his back, keeping him pinned to the floor. "Never touch her again," I snarl.

"Aidan."

I ignore Jason's warning as I extract a blade I always carry with me. I grip the hand that had touched Raven and hold it down on the wooden floor.

Patrick squirms. "Fine. Get off me, man." He tries to look at me, but I dig my knee into his back as I run the blade down his hand. His touching Raven isn't fine.

I push the blade down on his index finger. He screams as I sink the knife further into his skin. His howls continue as I slice the blade back and forth across his finger. My mind grows manic with revenge. He can't touch what's mine. I don't stop until the finger detaches and blood flows free across the floor. It's not enough. I want more, and as he continues to shriek, I push the bloody stub aside to carve another finger, when a hand lands on my shoulder.

"That's enough," Jason says with a calmness to his voice, but his gaze flickers to Raven, who's white-faced, with pure horror etched into her features.

Gilly isn't looking much better, but William smirks. "Now, this is what I call a party."

Each heavy breath I take doesn't calm my racing heart. My beast wants more blood, more fingers. I glance down at the severed digit, but it's not enough. Not even close.

"Aidan," Jason fires off again.

Patrick howls and cries, and I take one final look at Raven, who's covered her mouth with her hand. I want to scream at her. Look what she made me do. Just by being here, she's making me hurt people. First George, now Patrick.

I release Patrick's damaged hand and take my knee off his back. "The next time you even look at her, I'll take your fucking eyes out."

Patrick's eyes snap closed as he sobs. "I won't. I won't."

Good. I've made my point. And now it's time to end this party and get Raven out of my sight before she pushes me any further.

CHAPTER EIGHT

RAVEN

I CAN'T LOOK AWAY from the severed finger. My stomach twists and dips as my gaze tracks the trail of blood all the way to Patrick. He keeps his eyes closed, and a whimper spills from between his lips. Gilly reaches out to his friend. Aidan still holds the blade, and I fear his attention will fall on me. When Donald told me Aidan had requested me in the drawing room, I had feared that he was ready to punish me. Stepping into a room with several men, I thought I would be handed around. He had said I was only good for one thing.

Aidan's breathing heavily; his knuckles have turned white from the grip he has on the knife. When his gaze connects with mine, my heart thrashes so rapidly in my chest that I fear he'll hear the heavy thumping.

"Get him out of here," Aidan snaps while staring at me. His brown eyes appear dark, deadly, and demand more savagery.

"My finger," Patrick cries.

Aidan sneers. "Your finger is mine."

I'm ready to throw up. My mind's still processing George's death, like I can make sense of the violence.

Gilly grips Patrick, who keeps his eyes closed, and pulls him off the floor. Aidan had threatened to cut his eyes out if he looked at me, and I truly believe he would make good on his threat.

When they leave the room, William yelps. "That was fucking brilliant."

"Shut up, William," Jason snaps, and William obeys, the grin vanishing from his lips.

I flinch as Aidan steps closer to me. My ex-husband was vicious toward me. He liked using his fists or belt. But now I fear Aidan's violence is on a different level. I swallow as I glance at the blade stained with Patrick's blood. Will mine soon coat the blade?

Aidan's gaze hardens. I can't find a drop of warmth or compassion in it. When he steps closer, I want to run from him. I lock my knees so I don't move. My lips don't part to form any words.

Aidan wipes the bloody knife down his trousers before sheathing the weapon in his waistband. He takes one final glance at me before turning to Jason.

"He asked for it," he says as a way of explaining his actions.

Jason gives a curt nod, but he wears a look of disturbance I feel right down to my toes.

"Donald," Aidan calls, and I try not to jump at the sound of his sharp tone. Blood has pooled on the floor, and the severed finger grabs my attention all over again.

When Patrick trailed his fingers up my arm, I wanted to push him away, but I knew better.

I'm not aware that Donald has entered until Aidan speaks again. "Take Raven to her quarters."

Donald doesn't react to the disturbing scene before us. Instead, he holds out his arm. "This way, Miss Collins."

I try not to run from the room. I give Aidan a wide berth in case he changes his mind and tries to hurt me. No one moves as I walk out of the room with Donald. My stomach churns with each step I take up the stairs.

A bodyguard stands outside my quarters. I step across the threshold, and when the door closes behind me, I spin and swallow the strangled cry that has clawed its way up my throat.

Being in the company of that many dangerous men was terrifying. Watching my soon-to-be husband cut off Patrick's finger brought that fear to a new level. Would my father care if I told him? No, he wouldn't. I'm a pawn in his depraved game; I always have been.

My stomach protests again, and I move across the room to my bathroom, where I throw up the remnants of my earlier food. When my stomach continues to rebel, I don't stop heaving until every last drop of liquid leaves my system. Only then do I descend to the white marble floor. I'm waiting for the shock to pass and the tears to come, but they don't make an appearance. Instead, a memory of Victor assaults my mind.

"Little Bird, where are you?"

I sit up rod straight at the Russian accent that sends fear piercing through my system. The room is shrouded in darkness, and my heart jackhammers when I make out his silhouette close to the foot of the bed.

"Little bird, come out of your cage." The excitement in his voice has my hands gripping the quilt. He moves to the side of the bed, and before he even reaches me, the fumes of the alcohol have my eyes tightening. I know if I lie still, it will be over soon.

The covers are ripped from my tight grasp. His breath is heavy on my face. "Open your eyes."

The command has my eyelids snapping open. His large hand encases my cheek; the gesture could be mistaken for a lover's touch for all of a mere second before Victor's hand tightens on my face. There is nothing gentle or soft about Victor. He's cruel and enjoys the pain he inflicts on me.

"That's a good little bird."

I stand up, not wanting to remember the rest. I force myself to think of Louise creeping into my bed late at night, where she sought refuge from nightmares that kept her tossing and turning. I focused on her small body beside mine as she climbed under the duvet. Her scent of lavender tickled my nose while her soft blonde hair rubbed against my cheek. I would tuck the strands under her head and pull my sister closer to me. "You are safe now, Louise. Sleep." After I planted a kiss on her damp cheek, she would relax into me, and that's how we fell asleep most nights.

I change into my cream nightdress and climb into the queen-sized bed that's cold and unfamiliar. I don't know how sleep finds me, but it does, and I welcome the deep, dreamless slumber.

***

Waking up brings with it the memory of the severed finger and the loss of George. The image of Aidan holding the knife causes me to squeeze my eyes shut, like I can remove the horrible image from my mind. I can't. I climb out of bed. My foggy brain wants me to clarify that I'm safe. I'm alone in the room. I can't imagine anything worse than having Aidan beside me. I take solace in the silence for a moment before a knock on the door makes me want to crawl back under the quilts. I won't cower. I'm not that girl anymore.

The door opens without an invitation to enter, and Lily, one of the servants, smiles at me. "Good morning, Miss Collins." She's fluid on her feet. She reminds me of a dancer with how she moves quietly. She closes the door behind her and, without missing a beat, opens the heavy red drapes, letting light flood the room. The sun catches on her fiery red hair.

"How did you sleep?" she asks, moving away from the large bay window. She doesn't pause for a response as she opens the double doors to the walk-in wardrobe.

How did I sleep? I search for a word that best describes it. "Fine."

I didn't dream, but my nerves had jangled as I floated in a half sleep. I didn't expect any sleep at all.

"You will get used to the mattress, and your sleep will improve." She flashes a set of white teeth as she returns with cream pants and a royal blue silk shirt.

I don't think my sleep will ever improve, not while I'm under the same roof as Aidan. I wrap my arms around my waist to shake off the shiver. Every time I close my eyes, my mind replays Patrick's severed finger.

"Let's get you dressed."

I wonder why I have to get dressed. Do I have to be in his presence today? I know I can't hide in my room forever. I need to get the information for my father.

Be brave.

"Am I going somewhere?" My throat tastes dry.

Both of Lily's brows rise. "Master Aidan hasn't stated, but it's best to be ready."

I unfold my arms and go to my bathroom to wash up. The space is modern, and the white marble flooring continues the same theme along the countertops of his and her sinks. When I return, Lily has made my bed. On top of the duvet, she has laid out my clothes. She hums as she opens a window. I get dressed in the expensive outfit before slipping on a pair of cream-pointed boots that Lily must have retrieved while I washed up in the bathroom.

A knock on the door has my body growing rigid.

"That will be Rose with your breakfast." Lily strides to the door and lets Rose in. Rose gives me a curt nod before carrying a silver tray to a coffee table across from a large plasma TV. She sets out my breakfast. It's way too much for one person. The array of different breads, fruits, and cereals is unnecessary.

"I wasn't sure what you like, Miss Collins, so I brought a selection." Her matter-of-fact tone suits her. She has that no-nonsense appearance. She places everything on the table. "Tea or coffee?" she asks as she sets down a glass of orange juice before picking up the empty tray.

"A glass of water, please." My dry throat demands the cold liquid.

Rose leaves, and Lily picks up the remote, turning on the TV. The European news flashes across the screen in silence. The plush cream leather sofa offers me comfort as I sit down. I don't touch anything until Rose arrives back with a beaker of water and a glass. I try to quench my thirst, and after I empty the contents, Rose refills the glass.

"Thank you," I offer both Lilly and Rose.

I eat a few grapes and some mango while watching the news in silence. Rose leaves, but Lily remains. She enters the bathroom and stays in there. I assume she's cleaning. Once she finishes, she leaves me.

After a while, Rose returns and takes the breakfast plates away. I keep waiting for what comes next, but when I'm left alone, I try the door handle. It's locked, just like yesterday.

My lungs and mind crave fresh air. I open the double sliding doors and walk out onto the balcony. My room faces the back of the house. The pristine gardens below my balcony run close to the outbuildings that have some activity around them. Men stand guard as others arrive and disappear inside one of the large barns. I watch the activity for a while, until Rose returns with lunch. Only then do I go back inside.

The day fades away, but the image of the severed finger never leaves my mind. Each time a knock sounds at the door, my fear grows, but each time, it's only Rose or Lily. Lily continues with her upbeat attitude, and Rose seems to be responsible for feeding me while Lily cleans up and makes cheerful comments about the great weather or how pretty my room is.

I don't interact much, keeping my answers polite and to the point.

***

Days melt into each other, and I'm almost getting used to the new routine I've established here. But, I'm also getting itchy to get out of the room.

Lily's chirpiness grates on me as my longing for my sister grows heavier every day. My guilt over George's death continues to grow.

Today starts off the same as always, but as the time creeps closer to dinnertime, I know I need to see Aidan; I need to get information and get back to Louise. Lily enters like clockwork, and I'm standing, waiting for her.

An eyebrow arches up when she gazes at me.

"I want to see Aidan," I request. Everything about that sentence sounds wrong. I can't bear the thought of being near him.

"I'm sorry, Miss Collins, but our instructions..."

I walk past Lily and pull on the brass handle. I'm stunned when the door opens. I don't step out of the room but look out into the hall.

"Miss Collins, you cannot leave your room." Lily rushes toward me, and I make a rash decision and step out into the hallway.

"I want to see Aidan. I'm requesting to have dinner with him."

Rose makes her way up the stairs, carrying a tray of food. The moment she notices I'm outside my room, she stalls for a moment. "What is going on?"

Lily rushes toward her. "She wants to have dinner with Master Murphy."

Rose assesses me for a moment before she speaks. "Return to your room, and I'll see if Master Murphy is free."

My legs move far too quickly, and like a coward, I'm back in my room. Lily doesn't return with me, and when the door closes, I don't check to see if it's locked, because I'm certain it is.

Time wastes away, and I realize they've tricked me. No one will follow up on my request to see Aidan.

I'm pacing the floor when the door opens. It's about time.

I expect the arrival of Lily or Rose. What I don't expect is Aidan Murphy stepping into my bedroom.

What have I brought upon myself?

CHAPTER NINE

RAVEN

HE'S HERE IN MY room. I get a sense of the room shrinking as he takes a step forward. He has rolled his white shirt sleeves up all the way to his elbow. He folds his arms across his chest, causing the veins along his forearms to become visible. Tanned skin peeks out from the undone top two buttons of his shirt.

"You wanted my attention. Now you have it." He opens his arms wide, and when he takes another step toward me, I'm ready to sink to the floor. He cut off Patrick's finger, and he killed George. "What is it you wanted?" His gritty tone grows low and deadly.

I've made a mistake calling him here.

Think of Louise.

"I wanted to have dinner." My heart triples in speed as Aidan refolds his arms.

"I'll have Rose bring it up to you," he bites out. His brows furrow with a look of irritation at being disturbed.

A part of me begs to let him leave, to allow the silence to surround me once again and swallow up the words I need to say. Through the fear and trepidation, I find some semblance of strength. "I wanted to have dinner *with you*."

He glances at me from the corner of his eye before he turns away. His mouth drags up into an unfriendly smirk. He studies me, and with his head tilted, he strides closer. He said I was good for only one thing. My body tightens with that thought.

I clutch the sides of my dress like I can force myself not to move, not to run to the furthest part of my bedroom. The breeze slips into the room from the open balcony door and brushes the back of my legs. The crisp air steals some of the heat from my body.

"Fine. Dinner it is. I'll send Lily up to help you get ready. Until then, you stay in your room." Aidan glances around the space like it's his first time standing in here. The house is enormous, and I'm sure this is one of the many guest rooms.

I can't speak, so I answer with a jerk of my head.

He still hasn't left, and when he sweeps past, his cologne circles me, causing my stomach to squirm. I glance over my shoulder as he closes the balcony door. My heart sinks. Will it be locked like my bedroom door? He doesn't step away from the double glass doors but stares down at the gardens. His shoulders appear tense, and when he turns, his mouth moves, and I'm waiting for him to speak, but he doesn't. He walks past me, not leaving as much as an inch between us before he departs from my quarters.

I'm still rooted to the spot when Lily bursts into the room. She's all action as she pulls open the double door to my walk-in wardrobe.

"Dinner with Master Murphy sounds exciting." She's enthusiastic about the dinner as she disappears into the back of the wardrobe.

Dread floods my system, and the tsunami of emotions comes hard and fast. Lily returns with a royal blue dress. "This will bring out your eyes." She holds up the garment, and I agree with her. The color is almost the exact same shade as my eyes.

These aren't my clothes, but I know better than to object.

Once I'm dressed, I slip my feet into a pair of black high heels. "We should leave your hair down." Lily bows her head as she speaks. I like my hair down. It offers me the illusion of safety. With the dark strands pulled off my face, I'll feel too exposed. I give a quick nod in agreement.

"Sit down, and I'll help you with your makeup. All your scratches are nearly gone," Lily says as her gaze roams my face.

"No, I'm fine." I don't want to appear too eager with Aidan. He isn't a stupid man. The dress that hugs my every curve is overkill already, and once again, I'm very aware of his earlier statement about what I'm only good for.

Lily forces a smile. "Are you ready?"

No, I'm not. "Yes."

She beams, and I follow her out of my room. The bodyguard outside my bedroom door falls into step behind me. With Lily leading, we make our way downstairs and through the grand hallways of the mansion. Paintings take up a lot of space on the walls. Deep green floral wallpaper peeks out between the gaps. The gold trim along the architrave brings the small white flowers to life.

My nerves jangle with each step, but I know I can't hide forever. I need to do my job so I can garner my freedom.

You can do this. As we round a corner, I conjure the image of Louise to give myself courage. Servants push open the double oak doors, and I enter a grand dining hall.

My heart jumps as Aidan rises from the head of the table. The black slacks and shirt fit his broad frame. He's rolled down his sleeves, covering his tanned forearms. Dark hair falls into his black gaze. Running his hand through the strands, he pushes the hair back.

"Thank you for agreeing to have dinner with me," I say. I don't hold his gaze but take in the impressive, long dining table. The statement piece, which hangs above the table, a three-tier crystal chandelier, twinkles. Lily pulls out a chair to the right of Aidan. It's too close.

I try to bury my fear. This isn't new to me. I've done this once, and I can do it again. I take my seat in the red velvet chair and allow Lily to place the cloth napkin across my lap before she pushes me in. Aidan takes his seat again. I focus on the polished silver cutlery in front of me.

Silence has me glancing up. He's watching me. "You have a sister?" he asks.

The mention of Louise has me tensing. "Yes. Louise."

Aidan places his elbows on the table and leans in closer. The smell of his cologne wafts around me. My senses appreciate his scent. There isn't a blemish on his face. He's all angles and perfection. He's more suited to the front of a billionaire magazine than a member of the Mafia.

"How old is Louise?"

His question doesn't sit right with me. "Not of marrying age," I snap and want to reel my anger and words back.

Aidan's lip quirks up, and he removes his elbows from the table. He leans back in his seat, wearing a look of amusement. "I already have a bride." Something angry flashes in his eyes.

Is he disappointed? Do I care? "She's a child." I touch the cutlery to calm my nerves. I should tread carefully with Aidan, but at the mention of Louise, I seem to be losing any notion of self-preservation.

"Are you close to your sister?"

Sadness saturates me, and my hands feel heavy. "Yes," I whisper. The double doors into the dining room have been left open, and three servants arrive with trays of food. No one speaks as they lay out plates of salmon in front of us. More servants arrive and place steamed vegetables in silver dishes on the center of the table. When they all leave, I look at Aidan again to find him watching me.

He seems stiff, irritated, and that's the last thing I want to do to a man who cuts off people's body parts without blinking. I need to gain his trust.

"Do you have any sisters?" I ask.

"No. I have four brothers."

Dear God. Four more men like Aidan. The world would be a better place without them. Jason and William, I had met. Both are so different, but they all carry an undercurrent of instability about them. William seemed to be the most deranged; his enjoyment of watching his brother inflict pain made me sick.

"You've met William and Jason already." The moment Aidan speaks, his jaw tightens. Is he remembering what he did to Patrick?

"They seemed lovely." I pick up my knife and fork, but not before I hear him sneer.

I cut off a small piece of fish and chew.

"What about your other two brothers?" I ask.

Aidan picks up the tongs for the vegetables and places a bit of everything on my plate before filling his own.

"Thank you," I say.

"I have an older brother, Alex, and the second youngest is Matty."

The way he says Matty has me zoning in on that brother.

"Matty. That's a lovely name."

Aidan drops his knife and fork with a clank onto his plate, making me look at him.

"For someone who wanted dinner, you haven't eaten much."

I start to cut up my fish, hoping eating will satisfy him, but it seems to have the opposite effect. His features darken.

"What is it you like to do in your spare time?" I ask and hate how my voice wobbles.

He stops the pretense of eating and picks up his drink. "You ask a lot of questions."

My stomach rebels with every forkful of dinner I eat. "I'm trying to get to know you." The smile on my lips doesn't linger long. I struggle to hold it into place the longer his stormy eyes dance across my face.

"Don't. This is a business arrangement. You already know this." He takes a drink before placing his glass back on the table. "We are done here." He sounds bored.

I scramble, thinking of what else to say. "I think we should get to know each other, as we will both be living under the same roof."

He nods. "Why did you run?"

My heart pounds in my chest. Should I tell the truth to gain his trust? I follow my instincts. "I didn't want to marry you."

My stomach swirls from his abrupt laughter. His smile and laugh light up his eyes, and he looks alive. I hate how my body reacts.

"That was a very wise decision," he deadpans.

I glance at his hands, and once again, I'm thinking about how he severed Patrick's finger. "You didn't want to get married, either?" I ask.

He pushes out of his chair and rises. "Like I said, this dinner is over."

I rise, too; I can't let this end. Not yet. I need to get out of my room and start looking for the information my father wants. If Aidan won't open up, I need to look around.

"I've been locked in my room for days. I would like to have more freedom."

He nods. "Noted."

"Noted?"

"Yes, Raven." Aidan takes a step closer. He towers over me, taking up way too much of my personal space. "Request denied."

I'm pushing too hard, but I can't give up. "Will I be locked in my room for the entirety of our marriage?" The bite in my words has his lip tugging up in amusement. My cheeks heat.

"I haven't decided yet." He steps closer, and when he brushes strands of hair across my shoulder, I try not to flinch but don't succeed.

"I'm not the kind of person you want to get to know." His words wash across my mind as his gaze sweeps over my features. "I break pretty little things like you."

My mind spins, and I focus on the word pretty. He thinks I'm pretty. Then my brain skips to the part where he breaks pretty little things like me. *I'm already broken*, I want to tell him. His eyes harden, and I sense him shutting down.

I make a brash decision, not wanting this evening to end, so I rise up on the tips of my toes and press my lips against his. I'm surprised at how soft his mouth feels against mine. I'm surprised at the warmth I didn't expect. The moment doesn't last long, as he doesn't return the kiss. He grips my shoulders, and he pushes me away.

"That was a very bad decision," he grits out.

Dread pulses through my body, and I fear I've pushed too hard.

CHAPTER TEN

AIDAN

If Raven had approached me under normal circumstances, I would have taken her to my bedroom and had my way with her. But, nothing about these circumstances is normal. I push her mouth away from mine. Her cheeks darken from the rejection. She's also afraid. So I have no idea why she kissed me. It's easy to tell she doesn't want to talk to me, never mind press her lips against mine. Her actions show me her desperation. I want to know why. I want to grab her and kiss her just to see how far she'll go. But she's bewitching. She's dangerous.

"Tell me. If you didn't want to get married, what made you come here?"

She won't hold my stare. Wrapping her arms around her waist, her gaze darts all over the room, as if she might discover the correct answer. Just like she did while we ate. Everything about her answers is calculated, and I want to know why that is.

"I understand it's my duty," she settles on.

I grind my teeth at her well-rehearsed response. "One thing about me, Raven, is I don't like lies. You are lying to me." I step away from her, needing the distance. Everything about this woman entices me. Her smell, her striking blue eyes, the way she runs her hands along the side of her dress when she's nervous. I'm good at reading people, and she's terrified, yet something pushes her to bond with me.

"I'm not lying, Aidan." My name rolls off her tongue. She has no idea the effect she has on me.

Stuffing my hands in my trouser pockets, I force a smile. I'm sure it appears like a grimace. "So, your duty to your family is to marry me?"

"Isn't that your duty, too?" she fires back.

"Yes," I answer honestly. I know why I'm here. I know why I must marry Raven, but her wanting to have dinner with me and asking me questions isn't something she truly wants to do. She focused on Matty, and I wonder why that is.

Is she looking for the weak link in our armor? Matty would be just that. But Raven doesn't understand that my family will always come first. No matter how beautiful she is, it won't deter me from the path my brothers and I are on.

"I just wanted to have some company. But I can return to my room." She still won't look at me. Her focus rests on the open double doors that lead out into the hallway.

"Take a walk with me." It's clear she's surprised by the invitation.

This is her chance to leave. "Okay." She takes in a shallow breath. The pulse pounds along her neck.

"Let's go." I lead her through the hallway and into the conservatory. It's a heat trap that I never get to enjoy, but I can almost picture my father sitting in the corner on the woven chair smoking a cigar.

My body tenses as we pass his chair. An Aran throw, which is draped across the high arch, hasn't been washed since he last used it. Plants hang strategically from the ceiling, and the floor beneath is littered with a large array of potted flowers. I stopped watering them after he died, but I see the staff has continued on with my father's ritual. Sliding open the glass door, the warm summer breeze greets us, and when I flash a glance at Raven, the light wind stirs her long dark hair. She's skittish as we step out into the backyard.

We walk through the winding paths. The cloudless blue sky paints a stunning picture before us. The outbuildings are partially visible through gaps in the large oak trees that have been here for hundreds of years.

"It's a beautiful day," Raven chimes. Her voice shakes as she speaks. She clears her throat. "It's nice being outside."

I don't engage in conversation but allow her to rattle on about the plants and the large water feature we pass.

"You come from money," I finally say.

She stumbles, and I automatically reach out and steady her. She's pulling away slightly but thinks twice about the action. "Yes. My father owns hotels as well." Once again, she won't meet my eye. She's nervous.

"And casinos," I add, releasing her.

She tilts her head back to look up at me. I want to press on and find out what she really wants, but I can be patient. She just needs a reminder of who she's dealing with.

"Yes, and casinos. You also come from money." She's quick with the answer.

I grin at her. "Lots and lots of money, Raven."

I step closer and glance over her head at the outbuildings. "All built on the backs of others." I glance down, and she looks up at me. Her blue eyes widen. "Every euro is soaked in blood."

She shivers, and I know it's not from the warm summer breeze.

"I'm sure it's the same with your father, or he wouldn't have accumulated the wealth my uncle has spoken of."

"I don't know. I'm not privy to his business."

"Not that side of it, anyway," I say, and before she answers, I continue my walk. We close in to one of the large sheds. A man waits inside, a man who betrayed me and has to die as an example to the others. This is why I brought her out here, to let her watch what happens to people who disappoint me. To let her witness what happens to people who lie to me. As I take another look at Raven, I stuff my hands into my pockets with annoyance. I want to march her back to her room and lock the door.

"From my understanding, you make most of your money from buying and selling property." She isn't looking at me as she makes her statement.

"It seems your father shared our business endeavors with you, but not his own."

She shrugs. "I mean, I wanted to know who I was marrying."

More lies. Nothing about Raven adds up.

"The hardest part of this business is looking into a man's eyes"—I pause and grin—"or woman's, and knowing they are lying to you."

Her nostrils flare, and I know I've hit a nerve. I lean in close to Raven. "Do you know what happens to people who lie to me?"

She swallows and shakes her head. The long strands of black hair move viciously.

"I can show you." I point to the shed behind her, and she half turns. "In that shed is a man who lied to me, and he is awaiting his fate. What do you think that should be?"

She shakes her head for a second time. "I don't know."

I don't want to show her, so I give her one more chance. "Why did you agree to marry me?"

She isn't as quick with her answer this time. "To protect my sister." She looks up at me, and for the first time, I see the truth peeking out from behind her blue eyes.

"Aidan." Jason walks down the path toward us. When he joins Raven and me, he greets her with a nod. I know why he's here. I was in the middle of making an example out of Mark, who awaits his sentence in the shed, only I was called away by Donald. He informed me that Raven wanted my attention. I normally would ignore such a request, but inflicting pain on others doesn't come naturally to me, and killing takes me to a very dark place.

"Can you take Raven back to her room?" I ask Jason.

He's questioning me with his gaze. I'm sure he's wondering what she's even doing out here in the first place.

"Yes, you go ahead. I'll take it from here." Jason steps closer to Raven, who visibly recoils. A part of me doesn't want to leave her, but duty calls.

I have no departing words for her as I walk away and back toward the shed.

Mark struggles to keep himself from twisting. The chains around his wrists keep his arms pulled tight over his head. The tip of his toes dance along the ground as he tries to keep himself in one spot.

Three of my men stop talking when I enter.

"Where was I?" I ask as I walk up to Mark. I know what I have to do, and a part of me wants to make this quick, but like Uncle Frank said, a quick death doesn't leave a message; a slow, drawn-out one does. Today, I'm not in the mood to draw this torture out.

"You were telling me how you tried to sell my brothers and me out," I jog his memory, and that reminder gets my blood boiling.

"Aidan, they were going to hurt my family."

The three men snigger, as they already know Mark's fate. So does Mark. I will extract the information from him. It's really up to him how painful he wants to make this procedure.

My hand connects with his face three times. He doesn't cry out but tightens his jaw when I stop. "You know how this works. You tell me everything, and your family will be safe and taken care of." No matter how badly a member of our Mafia turns, their family will be protected as long as they stay loyal. One bad apple doesn't spoil the bunch once you eliminate it. But you have to remove the bad apple permanently.

His head hangs until his chin rests on his chest. "They wanted information on Matty."

I didn't expect that answer. Today seems to be full of surprises. I try to push the knowledge of Raven asking about Matty to the back of my mind. What are the odds both Raven and Mark want information on Matty?

Mark raises his head, his gaze hopeless. "I just had to tell them about Matty's movements."

I fold my arms across my chest so I don't reach out and strangle him to death. Matty might piss me off, but he's my brother, and the thought of someone wanting to hurt him has my restraint wavering. The shed door opens, and Jason walks in. Mark glances at him before his attention returns to me. "That's all I had to do."

"What did you tell the O'Reagans?" Four divisions divide up Ireland. The O'Reagans control the East, and they have family in the Northern Mafia as well. We control the South, but since my father showed weakness by taking his life, everyone wants to pick us off one by one. If it's not the O'Reagans, it's the Reillys or some of the Bratva, who have taken control of the South at an alarming speed.

Mark looks defeated and beat down, but I don't give a shit. I step closer and his mouth starts to move. "I told them where he would be tomorrow."

My heart skips a beat. He sold my brother out. We still have time to stop whatever the O'Reagans have in store, but only because one of our maids tipped us off after finding Mark in my office on my computer. He'd been checking our schedules.

"And where is that?" Jason asks, stealing all of Mark's attention.

Mark swallows, and his gaze darts between Jason and me. "That Matty would be at Glenlo Abbey Hotel with all of you for Aidan's wedding announcement."

Something so strong pierces my heart. We will all be under one roof tomorrow to meet Raven's parents. I'm sure the O'Reagans want to stop us from marrying so we don't strengthen our foothold. What fate would have waited for Matty at the hotel?

I don't get to react. Jason runs his blade across Mark's throat. A thin red line appears as Jason steps back, and seconds later, the blood starts to pool from the life-threatening cut.

I don't look away as Mark struggles against his chains. His instincts to grab his throat to stop the bleeding kick in. I watch as he starts to suffocate in his own blood, which spills from his mouth. I watch until the life leaves his eyes and he stops struggling. His body grows limp, and his feet drag along the ground.

"Matty can't go tomorrow," I say to Jason.

He sheaths his blade and gives me a quick jerk of his head. "I'll get Matty somewhere safe."

My men stand quietly. "Let this be a lesson to you. Spread the word about what happens when you cross a Murphy." The speech feels lifeless, but my men leave the shed. The blood still makes a pathway down Mark's shirt, soaking the material. Blood drips onto the concrete ground, yet it offers me no satisfaction. All I can think of is the fact our father was weak—so weak he took his own life, and in doing so, weakened all of us.

"I want Raven brought down here," I say.

"Why?" Jason asks.

I face my brother. "She was asking about Matty, and I know she's lying to me. What exactly about? I'm not sure. So I want her to see what happens to people who lie to me."

"You think she's spying on you?" Jason makes it sound like I'm paranoid.

"Something is off with her. She asked to have dinner with me."

Jason snorts. "That does sound suspicious." He walks to the side of the shed and turns the wheel, lowering Mark's body to the ground. "She's a girl who has to marry you, Aidan. I don't think you need to be suspicious of her." Jason continues to turn the wheel until Mark's body lies flat on the ground.

I dig my palms into my eyes. "She's afraid," I voice.

"She watched you cut off Patrick's finger." Jason continues to defend her as he walks back to me.

"Exactly," I bark. "Why have dinner with me? Why ask me questions if she's so fucking afraid? It doesn't add up. And why are you defending her?"

Jason doesn't flinch at my anger as he bends down and removes the chains from Mark's wrists. He doesn't speak until he's standing again. "You're focusing on the wrong thing, brother."

I fold my arms. "What should I focus on?"

"Your anger is misdirected. You are angry at what Father did. So am I."

I shift uncomfortably.

"Raven isn't the enemy here. She's just a means to an end."

I hate how that makes me feel. She's getting under my skin, and for the sake of ending the conversation, I exhale.

"We need to let Matty go tomorrow."

I laugh at Jason. "You just agreed that we need to get him to safety."

"In front of your men. What we need to do is let him come with us. He needs the break. They won't bother us now once the word is out."

I'm not comfortable with what Jason is saying, but I also see the logic in his words.

"I'll triple security," Jason says when I give him a doubtful look.

I forgot to tell Raven her parents will arrive tomorrow. Delivering that news gives me more joy than it should. I want to see her again, and maybe this time, I'll see how far she is willing to go. I don't trust her, but Jason doesn't need to know that I won't let this go. I will find out why Raven continues to lie to me.

With that thought, I leave the shed and make my way back to the house. Back to Raven.

CHAPTER ELEVEN

RAVEN

I CAN'T BREATHE. ONCE Jason walks me to the house and hands me over to Donald, I'm taken to my room. Standing close to the balcony door, I fight for air. I'm thinking about the kiss. *The one-sided kiss.* His soft lips and warm mouth sent waves crashing through my system. His scent still lingers. My face heats with the memory of Aidan pushing me away. My chest burns with the knowledge I hadn't been careful with my line of questioning. I need to pace myself and remember these dangerous men don't play around. My eagerness to get myself out of this situation forces me to make stupid decisions. With Victor, I asked questions at the right time. *Or so I thought.*

I pull open the sliding door to the balcony. Outside, the heavy air has me tugging at the neck of my dress. I focus on the garden; my attention drawn to the shed that Aidan disappeared into. A man waits inside that shed, Aidan said, and what exactly will Aidan do to him? I'm watching for a while when three men come out. From this distance, I can't make out their features. They all look intact. No one seems to be missing any body parts. I continue to watch for a while until the heat gets too much. I tug again on the neck of my dress but stop as Aidan appears.

My heartbeat starts to race as he walks across the lawn. His gaze clashes with mine, and the air halts in my lungs. I take a step back as he advances toward the house. When he disappears under the arch, I close my eyes and try to settle my nerves. He called me a liar. Does he know why I am here? No, if he did, I would be dead already.

I need to be careful with my line of questioning. Or maybe lie low for a few days and just request to have more freedom around the house. Once I find his office, I can start my search there. Befriending the staff would be wise since Lily and Rose spend so much time with me. Lily seems an easier target. With my plan in place, I feel a sense of calm. My illusion of serenity shatters when my bedroom door opens. The white linen fabric that drapes across the balcony door part from the breeze. Through the gaps, Aidan approaches. When the drapes settle, I panic when I can't see him until they stir again. He moves the fabric aside, and joins me on the balcony.

I fold my arms and turn toward the gardens. It's then I notice Jason leaving the shed. The closer he gets, the clearer he becomes. Is that blood on his shirt?

I take a quick glance at Aidan as he steps up to the railing of the balcony. His hands grip the rail, and I can't look away from his fingers. His hands are large, large enough to wrap around my neck and take my life away.

"I miss my sister," I say something that is honest since he keeps calling me a liar. He can't say I'm lying about that.

The sound of birds chirping and the warm summer breeze fills the silence between us. I unfold my arms and grip the railing, too. If he pushed me off the balcony, I would die. I couldn't survive the fall, and what would become of Louise? Would my father care if I died? Would he marry off Louise to clear his debt?

"The man who betrayed my family worked with us for half a decade. I've had barbecues with his wife, Sarah, and his daughters. I was at their wedding and had Sunday dinner at their home."

"I'm sorry," I say.

Aidan releases the railing and faces the doors. With his back to the garden, he says, "He's dead."

My stomach churns. My hand grips the railing until the pain in my fingers forces me to loosen my hold on the cold wrought iron and turning to Aidan.

Aidan moves closer, and I look into his dark deadly eyes.

I have no idea what he waits for, but he remains silent, staring at me. I step away from the railing, ready to return to the semi safety of my room when his hand snakes out. His fingers tighten on my wrist, freezing me to the spot.

He yanks me closer to him. "He's still in the shed. Lying on the concrete floor in a pool of blood."

A whimper I have no control over leaves my lips. I can't do this. The air grows thin as he pulls me even closer. My hand reaches out, and my fingers sprawl against his chest. The rapid beat of his pulse pounds under my palm.

When I look up at him, he's staring over my head. "I don't want to have to hurt you, Raven," he whispers. His gaze darts to my eyes before dipping to my lips. I take my hand off his chest and pull out of his hold with ease. "But, I will do anything to protect my family." His fierce words about protecting his family make me realize we just may have something in common. I will do anything to protect Louise, including marrying him.

He clears his throat and sinks his hands into his trousers pockets before glancing out on the garden. "Your family will be arriving tomorrow."

My heart thrashes in my chest, and a bud of hope blossoms, each petal unfurling with the rising joy. I'll get to see Louise.

Aidan steps closer to the balcony door. "You have access to the gym, library, and the main living room." He rattles off the rooms without looking at me. "Your door will be unlocked."

I shiver when his focus slams into me. "Don't go outside without someone." He enforces.

I don't care about going outside. My sole focus revolves around finding his office and getting my father the information. "Thank you."

He gives a jerk of his head before he leaves me.

I thought everything went wrong out in the gardens with Aidan and me, but clearly not. I must have gained some part of his trust since I can leave my room. I don't exit the balcony and into my room until the door clicks closed.

Louise will be here tomorrow. I can't stop the smile that graces my face. I'd get to see my sister.

***

I don't sleep much. I spend the night tossing and turning. A pounding headache greets me when I rouse from my unsettled sleep. My mind races through the events of yesterday. Staying out of Aidan's way sits at the top of my list. He sees too much. He's too clever, so I will get my information by scouring the house. Extracting the information from him doesn't seem like an option.

The door to my room opens as I push back the duvet. Lily smiles, and this time, I smile back. Befriending her makes it to the top of my list, as well.

"Good morning, Raven. How did you sleep?" She asks the same question every morning.

"Really well," I lie.

She beams. "What did I tell you? Didn't I say you would get used to the mattress?"

I throw my legs over the side of the bed. I might get used to the mattress, but I would never get used to this arrangement. "You did. And you were right." I stretch like a person would after a good night's sleep.

"I believe your family is arriving today."

Servants gossip. I know this, yet the oddness of being discussed settles around my shoulders. I shrug the sensation off. "I can't wait to see them."

"Your mother must be so excited."

My bare feet touch the cold wood. I wiggle my toes before I lie. "She's beside herself with joy."

I'm waiting for Lily to call me out on my lie, but instead, she claps her hands. "I'm so excited for you and Master Aidan."

She doesn't detect my deception.

"I'm nervous. I honestly..." I trail off and wave my hand in the air. "You don't need to hear my woes."

"No, I'm here for you. And I'm a really good listener."

I don't like being untrue to people, but I also don't like the idea of my sister being married off. "I'm nervous."

"About the wedding night?" Lily steps closer, her brows rise high.

"Well, that makes me nervous. But no, I don't really know Aidan."

"He's been in your room twice." She wrestles with a smile.

God, the servants do gossip. But they have no idea what goes on behind closed doors. If Lily believes Aidan and I have become intimate, then I will use that to gain her trust. I give a shy smile and dip my head.

"I won't tell anyone." Lily whispers. "I mean, it's the twenty-first century. You don't have to wait until the wedding night anymore."

The door opens, and Rose arrives with a tray of food. She gives Lily and me a disapproving glare. "I thought you would be dressed, Miss Collins."

"It's best that she has her breakfast first." Lily's quick with her reply. She gives my arm a quick squeeze before she progresses around me to make my bed. Rose's arrival kills our conversation, but at least I have made the first step in befriending Lily.

I take my seat on the black leather couch like I do each morning. The food forms a lump in my throat, and I swallow the toast with half a glass of water.

Today, Rose doesn't leave, and I have no idea why. She helps Lily tidy the room, and they both disappear into my walk-in closet. My lips tug up, and my throat burns. I can't wait to hold Louise and allow my mind to settle when I know she's safe.

Lily returns with a red full-length dress. The sleek fitted gown is draped across the bed. "I think for today, we will pin your hair up." Lily's eyes light up.

I prefer my hair down, but I also want Lily to like me. "My thoughts exactly."

Lily claps, but her excitement dwindles as Rose gives her a stern look. The shoes that Rose places at my feet seem a bit high.

"Could I have a smaller heel?"

"This is what Master Aidan has instructed. But I will happily get him for you." Rose's lips form a straight line as she waits for my response. Her tight features have me shaking my head.

"No, those shoes are fine."

She gives a quick jerk of her head before walking to my dressing table. Rose opens the lid of an oval oak jewelry box and removes a pair of small diamond stud earrings along with a large diamond encrusted necklace. I've been brought up around wealth, and I know that the necklace is extravagant.

"I'll just take a quick shower." I address Lily, who's fawning over the red dress. The long sleeves catch my attention, and I wonder how Aidan could know I like to cover my arms. Most likely, his picking that particular garment is a coincidence.

I strip off my nightclothes and walk into the spacious shower. The soft teal color palate in the bathroom gives the space a softness that my bedroom doesn't possess. The teal mosaic tiles under my feet shine with a gloss finish. I throw my head back under the spray of water. Light pours in from the overhead skylight, and I could bathe in the natural warmth all morning, but my excitement at seeing Louise has me washing with speed.

Once I'm done, I wrap myself in a plush teal towel that's trimmed in a soft gold. The mirror hasn't steamed over as much as a small instant fan keeps the fog clear. I blink at the girl, who looks back at me. A soft knock on the bathroom door draws me away from the girl.

I tighten the towel around my body before picking up a second towel for my hair.

"Raven, how nice to see you again." Gilly, Aidan's cousin, stands in the bathroom doorway.

The towel in my hand I grip tighter as my heart pounds viciously in my chest, and I glance around my room for Lily and Rose.

"We are alone," Gilly informs me.

Apprehension makes a steady path through my veins. His gaze travels down my neck and across my towel and when his gaze reverts on my face, something sinister flashes in his eyes.

CHAPTER TWELVE

RAVEN

GILLY'S MOUTH TUGS UP into a smile. He takes a step back, allowing me space to leave the bathroom. I don't make a move to enter the bedroom. I don't feel safe with him.

"Don't worry, the maids are busy cleaning up a mess downstairs."

I can read the rest of that sentence. A mess he must have made. "What do you want?" My voice sounds stable, unlike the tornado of fear and uncertainty that rips through me.

His smile melts off his face, and he runs both hands through his dark hair. "I like that, Raven. You want to get to the point." He turns his back on me and walks toward my bed. Opening a button on his three-piece suit jacket, he sits down while patting the space beside him. I stay rooted to the spot.

"I don't bite." He flashes a set of white teeth. "Unlike Aidan, who likes to cut off people's fingers."

The reminder of what Aidan did to Patrick should have Gilly nowhere near me. So it raises the question as to why he's in my bedroom. Does he not fear Aidan?

"I'm fine here." Another shiver runs the length of my spine as I speak.

He shrugs his shoulders and gets off the bed. "Did you know that my father, the head of the West Irish Mafia, set up this arranged marriage?" Before I can answer, he waves his hand in the air. "I'm sure you're wondering why he didn't marry you off to me, since I will be the next to rule." He side-eyes me.

I keep my lips tight together. I have no idea of the hierarchy of the Irish Mafia and have no interest in being educated on the matter.

"I wasn't a made man when my father offered you to Aidan. I'm a made man now." His gaze darkens.

I know what that term, made man, means; it's when you take a life. A shiver sends the hairs rising along my arms. "Aidan won't be happy that you're in my room." I grip my towel. The material strains against my hold. Water drips off the ends of my hair, splashing onto my cold flesh.

"Aidan won't be happy that he was given someone's sloppy seconds," Gilly bites back.

My heart thumps at the reminder of my previous marriage.

"Victor wasn't it? Aidan would surely kill him." His grin returns.

I'm the deer, frozen in the moment while I look down the barrel of a rifle. Water drips onto the floor, and I step out of the bathroom. I take two small steps to glance at the bedroom door. Come on, Lily and Rose. Gilly being here can't go unnoticed.

Gilly wags his head from side to side. "But then again, Aidan will kill you too. He won't want to marry the Bratva's leftovers."

My heart beats rapidly. "Are you going to tell him? Is that what this is about?"

Gilly's grin transmutes into a smile that isn't friendly. "That's up to you. I can keep a secret." He eliminates the space between us.

"What do you want?" I ask.

"You could start with a kiss." His hand snakes around the back of my neck, pushing my wet hair against my spine.

He leans in and I turn my head away. His lips land on my cheek. I'm bracing myself for his anger, but his menacing laughter causes me to glance at him. He releases my neck. "I'm sure Louise would be far more willing."

My stomach drops like a sinking ship. "Gilly," I say his name in a plea.

His hand snaps out, and he grips my face. My cheeks ache as he presses his fingers into my jaw. "If you don't do as I say, I will find a way to have your sister. I'll fuck her so hard she won't be able to walk." His anger is maniacal. He's unbalanced. Gilly releases my face, pushing me away from him. I stumble back but right myself before I fall over.

I want to ask why he's doing this, but I don't speak. I'm cautious as he paces in front of me like a man who has something to lose. What that is, I have no idea.

"You cost Patrick a finger." He reaches me again and pulls my hand away from the towel. I keep it tight against my body with my other hand.

"You have pretty fingers." He tugs my hand to his mouth, and revulsion pulses through me as he places my index finger in his mouth and sucks.

Releasing my hand, he leans in, and his breath brushes my face. "You do as I say from now on, and I won't tell Aidan that you are a slut."

My chest aches. I grit my teeth so I don't speak out of turn.

He taps my face twice with three fingers before spinning away. "We will chat again." He gives me a second look before he leaves the room. I want to sink to the floor when he's gone. My breaths are harsh and fast, and fear sends all the hair rising across my flesh. When the door opens a few minutes later, I can't keep still.

"A long shower I see," Lily chirps. She closes the door and pauses. "You look pale. Are you okay?"

I take in a large breath before tightening the towel around me. "Yes, I'm fine."

"You're nervous? That's okay. It's a big day." She beams at me. She brushes off my fear as a show of nerves. The pool of dread that whirls like a vortex in my stomach leaves me shaky.

"Let's get you dressed."

During the time I spend getting ready, my mind spins as I keep going over the conversation with Gilly. My father hadn't told me not to mention my previous marriage. I honestly wouldn't have, but now I know I need to keep that knowledge buried. Yet, how could something so big get past Aidan? Would he really kill me? My mind responds with a resounding yes. He would kill me. Then Louise would be left on her own or married off to someone like Gilly.

"You look breathtaking." Lily's words are low as she grips my shoulder and turns me to the full-length mirror. I've been so zoned out as she did my hair and makeup that I hadn't noticed we were finished. I didn't care what I looked like. All I cared about was seeing Louise and making sure she was okay.

My gaze rises from the red fabric that sits just a centimeter off the ground. A long slit up my left leg reveals a little flesh. The dress hugs my curves and stops in a cowl neck. The heavy diamond necklace sparkles as I shift slightly. The red sleeves are a touch I appreciate but also fear. They cover my past, a past I can't let Aidan see. My hair is pinned up off my face. I can't hide. Every inch of me, from my figure to my face, is on display. The dark gray eyeshadow brings out my blue eyes. They appear stark and I blink, glancing at Lily, who smiles behind me.

"You are so beautiful." She speaks with a whimsical tone.

"Thank you." I can't return the smile. I just want this done and over with. Finding the information my father seeks about Aidan is more important now than ever. I don't just need to get away from Aidan. I also need to get away from Gilly.

The door opens, and both Lily and I turn to Rose. "Your family is here." It's the first time I've seen Rose smile. It transforms her and I can picture her sitting in a kitchen that's filled with the scent of baked brown bread. A kitchen that is always open to visitors. At this moment she looks like someone you could talk to.

I run my hands along the side of my dress to steady my nerves and, without a word, I follow Rose from the room. Lily steps beside me and my body guard falls in behind us. I don't know why, this moment, as I walk down the stairs, feels so significant. Maybe it's how official this makes things with my family here, but more so, it's seeing Louise.

A smile plays on my lips, but I keep it at bay as we reach the ground floor. I'm led through the hallways and to the open doors of the main living area. This is the room where I first met Aidan, the room where he cut off Patrick's finger. I push that image to the back of my mind as I step inside. Everyone rises from their seats. Everyone but my father.

My gaze darts around at all the faces, but the one I'm looking for isn't here. Louise isn't here. My mother steps up to me and kisses me on each cheek. "You look beautiful," she whispers.

"Where's Louise?" I ask once she finishes pressing false kisses to my cheeks. She grips my arms. "At home."

"Why? With whom?" My voice rises.

My mother's eyes widen. "She wasn't up to the journey." The guilt shines in her gaze, and I want to push her hands off me. Aidan appears behind my mother, and she becomes aware of him, then lets me go. I'm aware of him, too aware. He's magnetic and so wrong. I didn't think anything could pull my mind from my sister, but my brain stalls at the sight of him in a black suit. His shirt is black; even his tie is black. Everything is as black as his eyes.

"Don't fuss, Raven. Louise is sick. We can't bring her here just because you say so." My father's words pull me away from looking at Aidan, the spell smashed to smithereens. His words are filled with mocking. He's done this on purpose. My blood boils, and I want to call him out.

"The food is ready." Donald speaks from behind me.

Aidan holds out his hand to me. "Shall we?" He sounds bored and won't look at me.

I don't want to touch him, but my father's gaze narrows, and I place my hand in Aidan's.

As we leave the living room, I can't help but notice how warm Aidan's hand is around mine. His touch is gentle, and when I glance at him, it's a contradiction to the tightness of his jaw.

"You have a beautiful home, Mr. Murphy," my mother sings. I hate her. I hate my father. I hate all of this. I glance back at my father, who also appears bored.

"You can call me Aidan, Mrs. Collins. And thank you. It was my father's," Aidan says, and once we reach the dining room, he pulls out a chair to his right for me to sit down. Aidan positions himself at the head of the table. My father sits at Aidan's left and my mother perches herself beside my father.

"Are your parents not joining us?" my mother asks.

My father moves quickly, covering her hand with his. She startles at the grip he forces on her small fingers. "I do apologize. My wife isn't around company much and has forgotten her manners."

I can't look away from the tightening grip he has on my mother's fingers. Her face twists in pain.

"It was a fair question, Mr. Collins. No need to apologize." At Aidan's sharp words, I wonder if my mother offended him. "But no, my parents will not be joining us."

Appetizers arrive. A waiter stands behind each of our chairs, and they all place Mini Beef Tourtières in front of us in sync.

Each time I think of Louise, my chest squeezes. "Is Louise sick?" I ask.

My father releases my mother's fingers, the skin white from the force he placed on them. "Are you not happy to see me and your mother?" He makes it sound like a joke.

"Of course, Father. I just..."

He waves me off. "Sometimes, Raven, you are exhausting." He laughs and reaches for a glass of wine that has been poured for each of us by another waiter. My father drinks his down before reaching across and taking my mother's. She's dropped her head, her focus on her plate.

"Please, eat," Aidan says.

Like robots, we pick up our knives and forks and start to eat.

"Master Murphy." Donald lingers at the doorway. "I do apologize, but another guest has arrived."

Aidan nods. "Can you bring me a fresh wineglass?" Aidan requests.

I meet my mother's gaze. She frowns. I want her to tell me where my sister is. I want to pry the information out of her. Isn't that what I'm good at? Didn't I practically sell my soul to Victor to get information for my father? Shame heats my cheeks before it spills over and turns into anger.

I'm angry. Angry enough that I can't even pretend to eat right now.

Donald and a servant arrive back. Donald hands Aidan the wineglass and the servant sets a place beside me.

Aidan rises and everyone watches as he walks behind my mother while holding the glass. I grip the knife and fork in my hand with fear at what he might do. Is he mad she spoke out of turn? I quickly look at my father, but he empties the glass of wine that he had stolen from my mother.

Aidan leans in and without a word, he places the glass in front of my mother before filling it half way up.

"Thank you." My mother sounds stunned, and I hate how I melt just a tiny bit.

Aidan returns to his seat, and footfalls behind me have me stiffening. They are not soft like a woman's. They aren't heels but the heavy footfalls of a man. The chair pulls out beside me, and I feel sick when Gilly sits down with a smile on his face.

"You must be Raven's parents. Can I say you have a stunning daughter?" Gilly's compliment falls on deaf ears. My mother stares at her glass of wine, my father, eating his food. I take a peek at Aidan. He's glaring at Gilly like he wants to murder him, and for the first time, I hope he does.

"This is Gilbert, Frank's son."

My father's head snaps up. "A pleasure to meet you." My father unbuttons his jacket and leans back in his chair. "You must be something to follow in your father's footsteps. Frank is quite the man." My father's praise irritates me.

"The pleasure is all mine. I can see where Raven gets her looks from."

My face heats and I hate how he keeps reverting to my looks. I want the ground to open up and swallow me.

"I don't recall you being invited." Aidan's words carry a note of loathing.

Gilly laughs and reaches for the wine. "Have you anything better than this?" His brazen tone surprises me. He wasn't quite so outspoken the first night I met him. A lot must have changed since then.

"Why don't we go down to the wine cellar and pick one out?" Aidan smiles, but it sends shivers down my spine. He wears a look that holds a promise. If you go to the wine cellar with him, there is a good chance you aren't returning.

"I'm sure this will do for now." Gilly pours himself a drink.

"You are Frank's only son?" my father inquires.

"One and only. No carbon copies of me." Gilly's voice fills with pride.

"And tell me, Gilbert, are you married?"

Everything in me freezes. What is my father doing?! I release the knife and fork before I damage my hand with the tight grip I have on them.

"I'm not. But, seeing how well my cousin is marrying, I just might consider it. Do you have any other daughters?" Gilbert asks.

My patience and tolerance splinter.

"Louise is not..." I want to say for sale, but I bite my tongue. "She's a child." My breaths come out harsh and fast. I know in our world fifteen isn't a child, but to me, Louise will always be a child.

Silence falls around the table and when I meet my father's gaze, I know I've pushed too far again.

CHAPTER THIRTEEN

AIDAN

I AM SO TIGHTLY wound up that I'm ready to snap. Gilly, the little bastard, thinks he can throw his weight around because he made his first kill a week ago. Ever since then, he has had this notion that he is somehow protected. He sits on a throne that no one can occupy but him, or so he thinks. Like fuck will that happen; over my dead body.

He can't be touched, but that doesn't mean I have to put up with his shit. If he wasn't Frank's son, I would have dragged him from his chair and away from Raven. Each comment has me fighting for control.

"Mind your mouth," Raven's father barks across the table at her, snapping me out of my reverie.

My fingers curl around the knife, and I think of every reason I could take his life right here at this table.

Raven's father drinks deeply. "You are a disappointment, Raven."

I release the knife because if I don't, it will be embedded in his neck.

I might not know her, but she's going to be my wife. "Mind your tone." I speak clearly. "She is to be my wife, and I won't have anyone speak down to her."

I meet her father's gaze. He's had far more to drink than two glasses of wine. He might be a man who likes his alcohol a bit too much. His false bravado dries up quickly, as I hope he remembers who he is in the company of. His wife looks so alive as she watches me reprimand him. He's a fucking bully, and it's clear as day that he doesn't mind hurting a woman.

"She needs to learn manners." His face reddens at being corrected.

He needs to learn some fucking manners. "Like I said, Mr. Collins. She's to be my wife. My rules," I declare.

His face darkens, but he wisely sips his drink. I don't look at Raven, I can't. I've never seen anyone so striking. She has the ability to make everything else disappear, and when she stepped into the living room, my heartbeat grew frantic. Not a feeling I'm accustomed to.

It's a reminder of how deadly her beauty is.

My gaze shifts to the gobshite at her side. I flash a warning with my eyes at Gilly; he isn't dumb, so he heeds my warning and eats his food. The appetizer is cleared away and the main course takes over. The conversation grows stifled, but I focus on Raven's mother. I ask basic questions, the weather, stories about Raven and Louise as kids, and if I wasn't seated close to two men I wanted to kill, I could almost think of myself smiling, and even laughing at the rebellious five-year-old that Raven was. She still has that streak. The defiance in her eyes still shines brightly. No one has put out that fire. The silly part of me hopes no one ever does.

"The room was white. I mean, I couldn't see one thing that had color. She emptied every bottle of talcum powder across the room. She looked up at me, and said, 'Mammy, it's snowing.'" Raven's mother smiles fondly at the memory.

"I don't remember that." Raven speaks for the first time, drawing my attention to her. She's frowning. "Why don't I remember that?"

"You were five at the time. All I could see were your beautiful blue eyes." Pain fills her mother's words.

"Jesus, Celine. You sure know how to kill a conversation," Raven's father speaks up. I can't do anything about how he treats his wife. It pisses me off, but it's also not my place to intervene. When the dessert ends, we take our drinks to the main living room. Gilly stays with us, and I'm sure Frank sent him to keep an eye on things.

Raven sits stiffly on the edge of the couch. She's seething. Each time she glares at her father, her blue eyes flare up. I could watch her all day. The emotions play so strongly in her eyes; she can't hide how she feels. Raven's mother perches herself beside her husband, who laughs along with Gilly. I stay standing at the fireplace. Jason appears in the doorway; before he enters, he gives me a nod in greeting. He steps into the room and Gilly grows quiet.

"This is my brother, Jason," I say to Raven's parents.

Raven glances at Jason, her body tensing before she forces her shoulders to relax. I take a sip of my drink as Jason takes Raven's father's outstretched hand. Once they all get acquainted, Donald arrives to fill up everyone's drinks and offer Jason one. He declines.

"The cars are waiting," he informs me.

Showtime.

Hundreds have been invited to this gathering. Some of the most influential people on the Mafia scene. We want them to see our strength. We need to make our mark. I know how important this day is. I place my half-empty glass on the mantelpiece. Raven's parents rise, but Raven remains seated.

She's like a foreign princess in a new land. I walk toward her, and with each step I take, she grows stiffer. When I hold out my hand in front of her, she stares at my fingers like they're lethal weapons. I suppose they are.

"The car is ready," I say to prompt her to take my hand. She glances at her parents. I don't know what she sees, but she slips her small hand into mine, and I help her to her feet. I don't release her hand. She tries to pull away, but I hold tight—not too tight to hurt her, but tight enough so she can't escape my grasp. We file out of the house.

Raven and I have our own car. The driver opens the back door, and only then do I release Raven's hand and allow her to slide in. The action has the split in her dress gaping, and my cock starts to grow as more of her thigh is on display. The moment she sits, she pulls the slit together, and I climb in beside her. The door closes, and the driver takes his position up front.

Gary, my personal bodyguard, gets into the passenger seat, and we set off for the hotel.

The back of the Range Rover is wide, and Raven uses the availability of space to create as much distance as possible between us.

My lip tugs up at her unease, but I don't allow the smile to form. "There will be a lot of people watching us."

Her head snaps toward me, her eyes wide. She exhales a long breath. "Like paparazzi?"

Her soft voice rolls over me. Everything about her entices me. "Yes, and a lot of business people. So, we need to show a united front."

She chews on her lip and nods before looking back out the window. I wonder what she's thinking.

"You need to relax, Raven."

She turns away from the window. "I'm trying." Her words are sharp. When I don't speak, she frowns. "I thought I would get to see my sister."

I've gathered that her attachment to her sister is substantial.

"Your mother said she was sick. Do you not believe her?" I ask. I didn't believe her parents. I am starting to see that Louise is a form of control over Raven.

"Of course I believe her." Raven runs her hand along the side of her dress. I've noticed her doing that when she's nervous or lying. "I just miss her."

"When we get home, why don't you call her?" I say.

Raven frowns again. "I can do that?" She appears perplexed.

I fight another smile. "Of course."

Her gaze travels across my face. "Thank you."

Irritation claws at my stomach. I'm not a fucking monster. Yet, she makes me feel like one. Her shock at being able to do such a basic thing like make a phone call pulls at my conscience.

I slip my phone out of my jacket pocket and scroll through emails, occupying myself for the next fifteen minutes. No matter how many times I read the messages, I don't take in anything. I'm too aware of Raven beside me. She shifts in her seat so many times. Her scent wafts around the car, and my mind replays the image of her thigh. I can picture both of them wrapped around my waist while I bury myself inside her. I put my phone away as the car starts to slow. Lights flash as reporters try to get a glimpse of us. But they won't capture anything through the tinted glass.

I take a look at Raven. She dips her head, peering out my window at the crowds that have gathered. Jesus, she appears petrified.

I move closer to her, and her attention shifts to me. The pulse flickers along her neck, and without thought, I reach across the space between us and touch her neck. Her lids flutter closed. I'm surprised at her reaction. When she opens her eyes, the blue is like the bottom of the ocean. Stunning.

My gaze drops to her glossed lips. The memory of the feel of them against mine has my cock growing harder. I had fought the last time not to kiss her back. I'm not sure I'd be strong enough to fight her again.

I'm aware of the driver and Gary waiting for the orders to get out. I release Raven's neck and turn away from her.

"Let's go," I say and within seconds, my door opens. I plaster on a blank expression as I step out of the car. Cameras flash in quick succession, and I turn, holding out my hand to Raven. She doesn't take it immediately. I know she's not trying to be fashionably late; she's terrified.

I keep my hand out, and she finally slides across the seat and takes my hand. I help her out, and the frenzy of cameras and our names being called demands our attention, but as Raven steps up beside me, my focus rests solely on her. I keep her hand in mine, and this time she doesn't try to pull away. More cars pull up, and security pours out of the second car. Three follow behind Gary, and the other two break off as Jason arrives. I meet my brother's eyes but stop on the red carpet. We might not have chosen this path, but it's one we're on and one we need to stay on. I pull Raven close to my side until she's tucked against me. Looking down at her, I lean in.

"I think a kiss would work well now," I say with a slight smile.

Her eyes widen and I don't give her a second to think. Am I kissing her for the cameras? Yes, but the pleasure I take in her soft, warm lips against mine turns the kiss into something deeper. Capturing her face in my hands, I taste her strawberry gloss, and when I move past that taste, it's the sweetness of wine that she drank.

"I think you can stop now." Jason speaks as he stands beside me.

I break the kiss and look at my brother, who poses alone for the camera. When his gaze meets mine, I see a question there.

Kissing Raven isn't exactly necessary. I release Raven's face, and she wears a dazed look. Taking her hand, we make our way into the hotel, ignoring all the calls from the reporters to answer questions about our upcoming wedding. Inside is calmer for a moment. It seems like every staff member in the hotel waits for us. They stand in rows on either side, every second one balancing a tray of flutes filled with champagne.

I pass them and don't stop until we reach the double doors that are pulled open for us. The noise is instant as the crowded room turns to us. Conversation ceases and everyone applauds. I allow myself to smile as I step into the room. I take a peek at Raven and am surprised to see her smiling. She still doesn't look completely relaxed, but at least she doesn't look half-frightened to death.

So many faces I recognize. Judge Caldwell greets me with a raised glass. He's kept us all out of jail and will continue to do so for a handsome sum. I spot Matty. He's on his phone, but four security men stand behind him. I know they are all carrying guns. I don't think anyone in this room isn't.

I shake hands and introduce Raven to solicitors, the mayor, and a few of the rich. When Richard O'Reagan walks toward me, I want to hide Raven. He's the head of the East Mafia. He also spent some time in a psychiatric ward. I spot Shay O'Reagan, another King of the East. Rumors have it he cut a man's head off and drove around with it in his car.

These men were born into this life. They know nothing different than killing.

"Congratulations are in order." Richard smiles at me. He gives Raven a quick glance. I still haven't released her hand, and I don't intend to. She is most certainly a sheep amongst the wolves.

"Thank you. I believe for you too. I heard you married Claire." This is information that's important to let him know we all have more than our lives to lose in this game. "I didn't get my invite," I say lightly.

Richard doesn't smile. "It was a private affair. Unlike you." He glances at Raven again. A waiter stops, and I take a champagne flute for Raven and hand it to her.

"Thank you." When she looks into my eyes, my gut tightens. She shouldn't be here—a showpiece to all these vultures. I want her to go home and back to her room. I release the glass and get one for myself. In the meantime, Richard takes one, too, as Shay walks toward us.

I've never met Shay before. He isn't like Richard. He doesn't wear a suit or keep a clean-shaven face. His beard is heavy, and the trousers and sweater aren't exactly the right attire for this function. He wears an air like he doesn't give a fuck, and I know why. He isn't just a king with the East; he also has power in the North because of who his father is.

As I stand before the two kings, I wonder which one put a hit on my brother. Shay holds a bottle of beer loosely between his fingers.

"Congratulations. You got lucky," Shay says before looking at Raven. He winks. "You pulled the short straw with him."

Raven's smile grows. "I don't think I did too badly."

Shay continues to smile at her, and I don't like it one bit. I know he has a girl who has never been seen. He keeps her away from all this, and maybe he's right to do so.

"We will chat later," Richard says before giving Raven a nod as he walks away. He's using this party to make his rounds. I think most people are networking. Shay doesn't leave.

"I need to use the bathroom," Raven says, and I reluctantly release her hand. I lean in and press a kiss to her cheek. She stiffens, and when I withdraw, she wears a smile like our kissing is normal. I think I need to give Raven more credit than I do. Her acting skills are very good. I watch her weave her way through the round tables that we'll occupy soon for drinks and light food.

"She is a beauty." Shay watches Raven walk away, and I rack my brain for the name of his girl.

"I hear Emma is too."

When Shay's face grows tight, I internally smile at getting her name right.

"I'm not going to beat around the bush." Shay folds his arms, and we stand shoulder to shoulder, looking out on the crowd. We both nod to people who greet us.

"I think Frank is making a huge mistake."

My hand tightens around the flute of champagne, but I remember my calm. "It's a good thing you don't have power in the South. Frank does." I nod at Jason as he passes me with one of the O'Rourkes. They are ruling the West of Ireland. We have better footing with them.

Shay laughs, but it's cut short as he spins so he faces me. I try to bury the knowledge that he cut a man's head off and drove around with it. "You think your old man opting out weakened you? You have no idea what the likes of Gilbert leading your family will do."

Everything in me snaps to attention. Gilbert isn't leading our family. Why would Shay O'Reagan think that? My mind spins, but I keep my calm. I can't show weakness. I step up to Shay and smile. "Why would you think Gilbert is leading our family?"

He tilts his head with a smile. "That's what everyone is talking about." He raises his drink and swallows deeply before departing. Panic starts to rush through me. I raise my glass and take another drink as I continue smiling and nodding at people. I scan the room for Raven, and when I don't spot her, my panic grows.

I motion to Gary with two fingers, and he walks toward me. "Find Raven," I say and keep walking.

Our security around the room is alerted by Gary, and they start to break formation from their stations. I leave the main room and walk down the hallway toward the bathrooms. I open the ladies' door, and several occupants spin and stare at me. No one says a word. None of these ladies are Raven. With each opened stall door, dread spins like a whirlpool in my gut. When I reach the last door, my heart sinks. She isn't here.

CHAPTER FOURTEEN

AIDAN

I'M STARING AT THE final empty bathroom stall. A heaviness in my gut surprises me. The fear isn't just that someone might be trying to stop Raven and me from marrying; the fear of losing her tightens like a vise around my neck. I have an idea of what these men are capable of. Men like Shay and Richard O'Reagan. Men like Dillion O'Rourke. The room fills with men who would kill without blinking.

Someone has just pulled out a royal flush by taking Raven.

I enter the hallway, and the sound of women chatting behind me resumes. Gary walks toward me. "Anything?" I ask, trying to keep my panic at bay.

He nods. "She's outside on the veranda." I move past him. "Stop the search. She has been found." His words drift after me as he communicates with the security team.

I keep my pace steady. I want to run, but I continue to nod and smile at the faces I pass as I make my way to the veranda.

The warm evening breeze greets me, along with a lungful of calm.

"There you are." I can't even explain the relief I feel at seeing Raven as she spins around to face me. But that calm evaporates as I see who she is with. Richard O'Reagan.

"I was keeping Raven company. You know, you shouldn't let her out of your sight." Richard takes a drink from his glass while glaring at me from over the rim.

I walk up to Raven, and on instinct, pull her against my side and away from Richard. She moves easily, not resisting my touch this time. I'd almost say she's finding comfort in my presence. I stare at Richard. "Is that a threat?"

He lowers his glass and grins at me. "It was an observation." Richard steps closer. "I'm not your enemy, Aidan."

I glance toward the double doors, where the party spills out. "You should tell that to Shay."

"Shay is just Shay." Richard waves his hand in the general direction of the party. No one comes out and joins us. Two of my security stand on either side of the door.

"I think Shay fears the monkeys are running the zoo," Richard continues.

I hold firm, knowing an attack on Richard O'Reagan wouldn't be wise, no matter how badly I want to hurt him.

He places his free hand in his trousers pocket. "Your father was a strong leader."

I can't stand the idea of him talking about my father. "So was yours," I fire back.

He flinches as if I've slapped him and removes his hand from his pocket, taking a step toward me. I move Raven behind my back, and once again, I notice how easily she follows my direction.

"My father was a bastard," Richard growls. "But yours wasn't. He kept a balance."

Is that respect I hear in his voice?

I can't stop the pain and uncertainty that rolls across my shoulders, tightening them. My father did keep a balance and a peace between the four different Mafia groups of Ireland. Now I wonder if Frank has reneged on that agreement.

"What exactly do you want, Richard?" I question and let a grin pull at my lips. I can't let him see he gets to me.

"I don't want a war. But Gilbert ruling the South isn't an option."

This, I agree on. I just can't understand what my uncle is doing. "I'm going to be honest with you. This is the first I'm hearing about Gilbert ruling the South. So someone is feeding you incorrect information."

Richard appears startled for a moment. He nods several times and takes a long drink before nodding again. "I hope you're right."

He walks away, and I'm left with an unsettling feeling. Why does he care if Gilbert rules the South? If having Gilly lead us would only weaken us, wouldn't that be to their benefit?

I want to let out a breath, but the warmth behind me has me turning to Raven. "You said you were going to the bathroom," I accuse.

"I needed fresh air." Her low tone doesn't hide the tremble to her words.

"What did Richard say to you?"

She won't look at me. I take her chin gently in my hand and tilt her head back, forcing her to look into my eyes.

"He spoke about the views around the hotel. And just asked me how we met." Her voice wobbles and I hope that's all. Richard knows this is an arranged marriage. Everyone does. I exhale loudly and release Raven's face. She doesn't step away from me, and I like how close we are. I take a quick glance at the party behind us before turning to Raven. The panic I felt at finding her missing was overwhelming. How can I feel this strongly about someone I just met?

She's bewitching.

"Do you think that's true about Gilbert?" she asks. But something else flutters to life in her gaze. Is that fear?

She glances away before I get to read more into her apprehension.

"No. I don't." I grit my teeth. Gilbert ruling better not be the truth.

Raven wears a look of relief, and I want to know why.

I take a step closer to her, and she tilts her head back to look up at me.

"What difference would it make to you if Gilbert led us?" What difference does Gilbert leading make to anyone other than me and my brothers? The next in line should be Alex. Now I wonder where he is and why he's never around. Did he see this coming and bail before everything got messy?

She shakes her head too quickly and runs her hands along the side of her dress. "It wouldn't."

She's lying. Why? I don't know. Her gaze lands on my mouth, and I let my lip tug up slightly. Her eyes snap back up to mine. The moment is perfect. My hand snakes around her neck, and I pull her into me, pressing my lips against hers. Raven's mouth moves under mine, making my doubts about her grow. She presses against my chest like she's ready to push me away, but she doesn't.

I run my tongue along her mouth, and her lips part on a small gasp of air. I slip my tongue into her mouth, my fingers running up into her hair, and I want to see the long strands spill down her back. My cock grows rock hard, and I drop my other hand until my fingers trail down and touch the flesh between the split of her dress. She inhales deeply at the contact. Her hands flatten against my chest, and when I break the kiss, she looks dazed.

She's breathing heavily. I don't remove my hand from her neck or thigh. "You sure know how to put on a show," she accuses.

No one is out here, only us, so her words annoy me. I take my hand off her thigh but don't release her neck. "You are a very good actress, too." I bite out the compliment.

Her cheeks darken. Her gaze falls to her hands, which are pressed to my chest. One at a time, she removes them, and I let her neck go. She wraps her arms around her waist. "We should go back in."

I'm not letting her off that easily. I hold out my hand and smile. "For the crowd," I say, but really, I like the feel of her.

She unwraps her arms and places her hand in mine so we can return to the party.

Some of the party goers have congregated around a poker table. Raven's father makes a lot of noise that's worked up the spectators. Raven's mother stands right behind her husband, a worried gleam in her eyes.

I keep Raven's hand in mine, her fingers tensing the closer we get to the table. Waiters arrive and replace empty glasses with full ones. I accept a drink for myself and Raven. I don't drink from my glass; I need to keep a clear head, especially after Shay's and Richard's warnings.

"All in," Raven's father announces, pushing his chips to the middle of the table. Two people drop their cards and declare themselves out. One other player remains and matches Raven's father's chips. Tension grows, but I take a quick look around the room and spot Matty still on his phone, with his entourage of security around him. At least he's safe. I haven't seen William or Alex, but I'm sure they've made an appearance.

I spot Gary and jerk my chin toward him. He weaves through the crowd and stops at my side. "Stay with Raven." I release her hand. "Don't let her out of your sight," I say before facing Raven. She's watching me. I lean in and brush a kiss against her cheek. "I won't be long."

I walk across the room to Jason, who's stepping away from Dillon O'Rourke. I place the flute of champagne on the table behind us.

"I had an interesting talk with Shay and Richard O'Reagan."

"I saw that," Jason comments.

"They're under the belief that Gilly is next to take over the South." I watch Jason carefully for a reaction to this news.

He snorts a laugh. "I highly doubt that."

Commotion at the main doors garners everyone's attention. Frank and his wife, Isabella, have arrived.

"I'll go to the source and ask, shall I?" I say, picking up my glass, and I'm ready to walk off when Jason grabs my forearm.

"Be careful with your words." My brother's low tone causes me to face him again, and I want to know what he isn't telling me. I keep my gaze on Frank as he greets people, and his wife smiles for the crowds.

"I always am," I say and walk away from Jason. I spot William at a table with three ladies. They are all engrossed with whatever tall tale he's spinning. His eyes dance with alcohol. I'm tempted to turn back to Jason and tell him to keep an eye on William, when I see him approach William's table and pull out a chair. Good, at least William will be kept in check.

"The man of the hour," Frank greets me. I take his hand and shake it before turning to his wife. I place a kiss on both her cheeks. "You look beautiful." The golden dress sparkles under the hundreds of lights that shine from the ceiling.

She smiles fondly at me. "And you look dashing." She quirks a dark brow.

Isabella is Frank's third wife, and she knows how to play the game, so I'm sure she'll be around for a while, unlike his last two wives.

"I was wondering if I could have a word," I say to Frank, my eagerness to crush the rumors catching up with me.

Frank leans in and pats me on the arm. "In time. I have an announcement to make." Frank passes me with smiles and greetings, and I'm left more unsettled. I spin, watching him make his way to the front of the room.

My gaze settles on Jason, who's watching me. I shake my head to let him know I got nothing out of our uncle.

A small podium at the front of the room becomes Frank's focus, and when he steps up onto the platform, he holds a glass in his hand. "Ladies and Gentlemen, welcome."

Everyone settles and I slowly make my way to Raven's side. Gary stays with us as we all look at Frank.

"Today is the first day of something great," Frank starts. His attention narrows on me and Raven. "My nephew will marry, and that union is very welcome after some troubling times." Frank pauses and his face grows drawn. "My brother, as you all know, was a fierce leader." He pauses again to allow his words to sink in.

"To Edward, or as most of you called him, Eddie." He raises a glass to our father, and we all do the same. "Onto happier times, for Aidan and Raven." All eyes turn to us, and I drink to that but don't look at Raven. Something tells me that Frank isn't done. His gaze travels across the crowd, and a knot twists in my gut.

"Gilbert, come here." The crowd parts to the left of the room, and I don't see Gilly until he steps up beside his father. He's all dressed in black and holds himself with an air of importance. His father extends one arm, and Gilly steps closer to Frank. "My son, Gilbert, is also a formidable man."

He's a fucking jackass.

"One who will rule the South well." The crowd lets out an inaudible gasp.

My gaze clashes with Jason's. Did he know? The O'Reagans were right. The shift in the room tells of a forthcoming storm. Like when the clouds darken before the sky opens and spills down on its victims.

"So raise your glass to the next leader of the South." The glasses rise slowly and with uncertainty, but Gilly doesn't see the hesitation in the rich and powerful hands as he smiles out on the crowd.

"To Gilbert," Frank reinforces.

The repeats of Gilbert's name are low, and everyone drinks.

"Now have some fun," Frank declares before stepping off the podium, and my mind spins. Gilbert being placed as our leader is the worst move ever. But Frank isn't stupid; at least I never thought so.

"My daughter may be marrying the wrong man." Raven's father sneers beside us, and I'm not the only person who tenses; so does Raven. My patience snaps.

I'm going to kill him. I spin and I don't know what makes me pause—maybe the fact that everyone is watching us, and striking Raven's father isn't wise.

"What exactly are you trying to say?" I manage between clenched teeth.

His eyes are bright and shine with all the alcohol. He doesn't seem to notice how many people watch us as he smiles up at me. "I'm saying you better watch yourself, or else."

CHAPTER FIFTEEN

RAVEN

THE AIR HALTS IN my throat. This evening has been a nightmare. My pulse pounds faster with each passing hour. Aidan tightens his fists as he steps up to my father. People around us watch. My father pales, but I think it's too late for him to save himself. Why would he threaten Aidan? None of this makes any sense.

"Or else what?" Aidan sneers. Aidan is a ball—no, a mass—of anger and tightness. My instincts tell me to run and find cover before he unleashes his wrath. He killed George. Does my father know that? He cut off Patrick's finger. Aidan is capable of unspeakable actions. I hate my father, but I don't want to witness his death either. I swallow my fear.

"Father..." I try to interject so they don't cause a bigger scene than they are already causing.

My father pins me with a venomous stare. "Be quiet."

"You speak to her like that one more time, and I will tear your head from your shoulders," Aidan growls.

The room spins with Aidan's threat, and some sick part of me wants to watch Aidan make good on his promise, while another feels sickened by the level of violence. My mother stands to my father's right, and I see it so clear in her eyes. She wants to witness Aidan hurting my father, too.

"Gentlemen, let's all take a moment." Frank places an arm around my father's shoulders.

"I meant what I said." Aidan isn't backing down.

My chest swells and my throat burns. He may be showing his dominance for the Mafia crowd, but some tiny part of me likes to think his fierce posturing is for me.

"He will learn to watch his tongue." Frank's reassurance is delivered with an arm placed on my father's shoulder. "Isn't that right, Gerry?"

My father's color trickles back into his cheeks; the redness grows deeper and spreads like a vicious virus across his forehead. My father nods in agreement. Frank smiles and glances at Aidan. "See, all is sorted."

"No, it's not," Aidan snaps. His hands squeeze into tight fists. "I want him to apologize to Raven."

All gazes swing to me, and I hate the attention. I run my hands along the side of my dress, and it calms the frantic frenzy that pulses inside me. My father has never uttered an apology in his life, so I'm sure I'll witness his death at the hands of Aidan.

My father scoffs and gives Frank an incredulous glance.

"I think it would be fitting to apologize to your daughter," Frank encourages before removing his arm from around my father's shoulder. The action makes me think of how Frank has taken a protective blanket off my father, and now he stands in front of wolves. His humiliation is already going to leave an ugly scar. Apologizing will come with its own set of consequences.

I hold my head high and wait for the apology. Aidan's hand snaps out toward my father's throat, and my heart jumps at the abrupt movement. Aidan grabs my father's gray suit jacket. "Apologize," Aidan demands.

The room disappears around me, and all I take in is my father's reddening face. His gaze lands on me, and the look in his eyes promises my bloody murder. "I'm sorry."

Aidan doesn't release my father but shakes him while wearing a smug smile on his face. "Raven."

My father's jaw tightens. Aidan makes sure he humiliates him. Guilt churns in my belly at how happy that makes me. I shouldn't want him to be humiliated. I just want to live my life away from him.

"I'm sorry, Raven," my father growls out.

Aidan still hasn't released him. He doesn't appear to be even half done, but Frank touches Aidan's hand that holds my father tightly. "Aidan," he warns.

Aidan's fingers uncurl from my father's suit jacket.

"Now Gerry, why don't you take your wife and get her a drink?" Frank smiles like this was just a minor disagreement and not death threats being flung around.

My father spins away, and my mother yelps as he grips her arm, dragging her with him. I bite the inside of my cheek, hating how I can't help her. Everything in my body is so tight that blinking is almost painful.

"You need to keep your temper in check." Frank speaks to Aidan while looking out onto the main floor.

Aidan loosens his fists. He turns to Frank. "We need to talk."

"We will. But for now, enjoy your party." Frank leaves, but Aidan doesn't move straight away. When he finally does, his full attention bears down on me. The wrath in his gaze makes me flinch. Have I got it all wrong? Will his anger spill out onto me?

"Are you okay?" he asks, and I hate how he keeps surprising me. I hate the swirl of excitement that spins in the pit of my stomach each time he looks at me. I drop my gaze. That kiss nearly had me fooled. I thought, for just a moment, that he meant that kiss, until I remembered this is for show. When will I learn? Women are pawns in men's games.

"Yes." I hold my head high and track my father, who whispers words into my mother's ear. Her shoulders hunch with fear.

I can't stand by any longer. I start to walk toward them, but a gentle hand grasps my wrist. "Raven, now is not the time," Aidan whispers close to my ear.

I'm so angry with how we're treated. I spin so I'm facing Aidan. "You think I should stand by and watch him abuse her?"

Aidan glances over my head, in the vicinity of my parents. "I think the abuse has been going on for a very long time."

"That's not what I asked you," I bark. I swallow when Aidan glances down at me, his fingers tighten around my wrist.

"No, I don't think you should stand by and watch him abuse your mother," he says. I'm ready to walk off, when Aidan pulls me closer to him. "I won't stop you from going over there, but if he touches you, I *will* kill him."

Aidan releases me and my breaths become heavier as I really let that information settle. I want my father out of my life, but to know that my actions would allow Aidan to kill him makes me as bad as these men. Tears of frustration burn my eyes, and when I look back at my parents, my father is nowhere in sight. My mother nurses a drink.

A man walking toward us captures my attention. He has Aidan's eyes and a strong nose. His square jaw mirrors Aidan's. He runs a hand through his thick, dark hair before he reaches us. I take a peek at Aidan. His shoulders are squared as he takes the hand of the man who steps beside us.

"Alex, I didn't think you had time to come." Aidan's words are filled with loathing.

"And miss the function of the week?" Alex smiles, but there is nothing nice about it. He's extremely handsome, just like Aidan—just like all the Murphy brothers.

"You must be Raven Collins." Alex releases Aidan's hand and reaches out to me. I take his large fingers and give his hand a quick shake. "I'm Alex, Aidan's big brother."

"You look so alike," I find myself saying and release his hand. It's intimidating being sandwiched between these two men who could be on the front of some vanity magazine.

"Don't say that," Aidan teases, but his voice still holds onto his anger.

I try a smile out, but I don't think it lands. Aidan looks away and nods at someone. That someone is Gary, his bodyguard, who has stayed with me since I went out on the veranda earlier.

"Could you take Raven to the bar and get her drink?"

In other words, he wants me out of earshot. Gary holds out his arm, and I walk toward him.

"Lovely meeting you, Raven. I'm sure we will catch up properly back at the house."

I manage a meager smile before I follow Gary to the bar. My mother nurses her drink, and I slide up beside her.

I'm waiting for her watery eyes to focus on me, but I'm greeted with a huge smile, her gaze alight. I've never seen her look so alive.

The bartender arrives in front of me. I don't want alcohol, so I order a tea. He doesn't question my choice but leaves.

"You want to tell me why you're smiling?" I ask.

My mother continues to smile. "We hit the jackpot here."

I glance around the room. No expense has been spared. I overheard a guest say that the gold rim on the plates is twenty-four karat gold. The amount of staff is overkill. I'm sure there is a waiter for every five guests, and the guest list ran into the hundreds.

"We have a lot of wealth, too," I say while I watch my mother. She must know we are bankrupt. She shifts closer to me.

"No, with Aidan. He stood up to your father." Her eyes appear feverish with excitement. My mother raises her glass and takes a large drink before smiling at me. "You need to make your father hit you, then Aidan can..."

'Kill him' I'm sure is the rest of that sentence. The bartender arrives back with my tea, milk, and sugar. I prepare my tea but stop and meet my reflection in-between the stacked bottles on the mirrored wall. My gut squeezes.

"You and Louise wouldn't have to run, Raven." My mother's smile melts off her face, her gaze shimmering with emotion. "We could all stay together. Me, you, and Louise."

I'm drowning in this moment. I want to say yes. What she says makes sense. But it's not the question of Aidan killing my father; it's the question of having my mother remain in my and Louise's life.

"Louise deserves better than you." My fingers tighten around the packet of sugar as I speak my truth.

My mother flinches. Her lip drags down; she runs her hand along her pearl necklace. "Fine. You and Louise can leave." She won't look at me as she gives us up without a fight.

A lone tear escapes, and I wipe it away. "If I do this, you will never see us again." I want her to say, no, that she won't agree to it. That she could never lose her girls.

"Okay." She finishes her drink as I try not to allow the sense of abandonment to show on my face. The real reason I'm doing this is that I won't have to betray Aidan, either. I won't have to get my father's information if he's dead.

My stomach roils, and I remind myself that I'm not the monster here, no matter what my conscience tries to convince me.

The party continues, and I keep an eye on my father as I sip my tea. He avoids me, not giving me an opportunity to put my plan into action.

Honestly, I'm so emotionally spent tonight that rolling my plan into action won't work. Aidan leaves Gary with me for the rest of the party. When he returns to me, the small things burn my flesh. Like how he places his hand on my lower back, his thumb flicking back and forth in a soothing motion. How the scent of his cologne consumes me each time he is near, or the quick kisses he brushes against my cheek. I don't recoil from them but find an ease with Aidan. That is, until I meet his heavy gaze.

"You look tired. Why don't you go home and rest?"

Funny how a part of me doesn't want to leave him. I dip my head so he can't read my gaze. "Great," I say.

"Take Raven home and stay with her," Aidan instructs Gary.

I could have used this as an opportunity to search the house, but if I play my cards right, I might not have to do this anymore. Excitement bubbles in my belly, and with the glee that glows within me, I smile up at Aidan. "Good night."

He frowns for a moment before leaning in. The kiss he brushes just at the corner of my mouth lingers, and my eyelids flutter closed. One minute I'm consumed with everything that is Aidan; the next, he's gone, taking his warmth and scent with him.

"The car is ready." Gary speaks on my left.

I go to leave the party, but before I do, I take one final look at my mother. She's still at the bar, still drinking. She doesn't see me leave.

Outside, the air bites any exposed flesh, and I hurry into the back of the car as the driver holds the door open for me. Once I'm in, he closes me inside. Gary gets into the passenger seat, and we pull away from the hotel and make our way back to Aidan's home.

When we arrive at home, Gary and Donald lead me upstairs. I don't mind being restricted to my room. The moment the door closes, I have a second of appreciation for Rose and Lily. A plate of sandwiches, along with a juice, has been placed on my table.

I kick off my high heels and advance toward the sandwiches. I'm ready to peel off the cellophane that's wrapped around the plate when the hairs rise on the back of my neck. I can't pinpoint why I have this sense of fear. I glance around the room, and my gaze returns to the curtains that are dragged across the double doors that lead out to the balcony. They shift slightly.

With my heart in my mouth, I take a step toward them. My pulse pounds as a hand snakes through the curtains and pulls them aside. Anxiety anchors itself in the center of my stomach. I'm looking into eyes that pull a whimper from my lips. My eyelids flutter closed. I don't want to be here. I can't do this.

CHAPTER SIXTEEN

RAVEN

"PLEASE," I BEG, KEEPING my eyes closed. I tighten my hands into fists along my sides.

"Open your eyes." Gilly touches my chin, and my eyelids snap open. His touch makes me shiver.

He taps my cheek with no force, yet it reverberates all the way down to my soul. His fingers trail across my face, and I whimper again. He laughs.

"Please," I repeat.

He grabs my lips and pulls them painfully. "Hush." He releases me, and my tongue flicks out to try to stop the sting that burns my mouth.

"Did you hear the announcement?" He walks away from me, and I have a moment of reprieve, but it doesn't last long. He sits down on the couch and opens the sandwiches. He eats a full one before looking at me. I realize I haven't answered him. I'm sure he's referring to the announcement that he will rule the South next. That makes him more dangerous than Aidan.

"Yes. Congratulations."

He pats the couch beside him while stuffing a sandwich into his mouth. When I don't move, his gaze narrows. I want to beg him to not do this, but I walk across the floor. I sit down as far from him as possible. He offers me a sandwich, and I decline with a shake of my head.

His arm is strewn across the back of the couch, and he drops his hand. "I saw you were ready to devour the sandwiches when you came in, so eat."

I take the small triangle of bread between my fingers and take a bite.

"I'm not sure what to do first. Should I rock the boat a bit?" Gilly grins. "Let Aidan and his brothers clean up my mess?"

Gilly eats another sandwich and nods at me, his gaze dancing from the sandwich that's flattened between my fingers and my mouth. When his gaze stays on my mouth, I stuff half the sandwich in and start chewing. He looks away, picking up the juice and emptying half the contents. When he's done, he offers me the bottle.

I want to decline but accept. I turn the bottle so my mouth doesn't touch where his did. He laughs at me, and my heart roars. When he rises, I'm waiting for the backlash, but instead he walks around my room.

"I would have made you my wife, Raven. I mean..." He glances at me and clicks his fingers. "I could have you in the blink of an eye."

The question that hangs in the air is, so why isn't he? Or is this the moment I find out that I'm not marrying

Aidan? Why does that hurt so much? I screw the lid onto the bottle and place the juice on the table.

"But marrying you comes with too much trouble." He grins at me and pauses as he takes a step toward me. "What a pity."

What trouble?

He returns to the couch, and this time he leaves no room between us. "My stomach is full. What else does a man want?"

The hairs rise all over my body.

"Why don't you start by getting on your knees?" Gilly fluidly pushes his hips up and pushes down his trousers and boxers. His cock springs free, and my heart triples in speed. This can't be happening.

He strokes his erection a few times. "Your mouth better be on my cock in a second, Raven." He trails off, not finishing his threat.

Bile claws up my throat. I can't do this. I'm shaking my head vehemently.

Gilly's gaze darkens, and he flashes me a warning before speaking, "If you don't start..."

He doesn't have to finish that threat. I reach out and notice how badly my hand trembles. When my hand touches his meaty flesh, he sighs and removes his hand. I glance at the darkened TV screen, and I focus on the depth of the blackness. My reflection haunts me, but I pick a dark spot and wonder how many black dots make up the TV.

"Oh, yeah, stroke that, you little bitch," Gilly says.

My hand moves on autopilot, running up and down his shaft. I move faster. My gaze keeps snagging on my red dress, but red is not the color we need to focus on. It's the black, the black of the TV. So black. I blink and a tear spills.

Gilly groans and I move faster, my timing perfect. I move faster and harder, ready to end this madness.

"Look at me, you slut."

Fuck.

"Get down there and use your mouth. Or your sister will."

I don't know why, but my messed-up mind starts to picture her, with tears pouring down her face while Gilly rams his cock down her throat. I release his cock as tears stream down my face. I'm glaring at his cock, and a grin twists my lips as tears continue to stream.

I take the head of his cock in between my lips and snap my mouth shut. My teeth sink into his flesh, and I don't stop until my teeth are almost touching.

A fist connects with the side of my head. I don't release his cock as his hand sinks into my hair and he pulls, ripping strands from my head. He has no idea of the beatings I took from Victor. He has no idea of my endurance.

His fist connects with the side of my head again, and this time, I release him and fall back onto the floor. My hearing grows fuzzy, and he stands up, turning away. His head is bent as he checks the damage. I taste the blood in my mouth and, like a sickness, I swallow the liquid like a prized wine.

I earned his blood. Gilly spins toward me, but my hearing still hasn't returned. He zips up his trousers. Gilly's gaze snaps forward, and he's running for the balcony doors. He disappears. A sob chokes free from my lips. The glorious feeling of hurting him ebbs away. He is to be the leader of the Mafia, and he did threaten Louise's life. I sit, only to have the room spin. Hands touch my shoulders, and I jerk away but relax as Lily pats me softly.

She doesn't ask me what happened. She helps me off the floor and to the bed. My stomach clenches, threatening to rebel against the contents I consumed at the party.

"Let's get you ready for bed." Sound returns, and I nod at Lily as she strips me out of the dress. I'm numb for a moment as she returns with my nightclothes. I get dressed while my head continues to throb. The consequences of my actions will no doubt be severe. I should feel more panicked than I do. The rebellious part of me is elated.

Lily pulls back my duvet, and I climb into the bed. She shifts around the room and when she locks the balcony door, I remember that's where Gilly had gone.

I climb out of bed.

"Are you okay?" Lily asks.

I pull back the curtains and unlock the doors but don't pull them open. What if he's out there? What if he throws me over the balcony?

"Are you okay, Raven?" Lily joins me at the door. "Did you hear something?"

I nod.

She touches my hand that still grips the door. When our gazes meet, she nods at me. "Let me check."

It's selfish of me, but I remove my hand and step back, allowing Lily to possibly walk straight into danger. My hands run up and down the side of my nightdress and wait for her screams as I picture Gilly shoving her across the railing. And what will I do? Stand here and allow that to happen? That's not who I am. In a sheer panic, I step to the door when Lily's face reappears. She blocks me from leaving.

"There is nothing out there."

I swallow my guilt and let her into the room. She relocks the door and pulls the curtains over. On autopilot, I climb back into the bed. My mind makes me believe that I'm dreaming. None of this can be real. Lily disappears into the bathroom, and when she returns, she holds a washcloth in her hand.

I'm confused for a moment until she brushes the side of my mouth. When she steps back with the washcloth in her hand, I see the smear of blood.

She doesn't ask what happened. "Good night, Raven." She walks away and takes the washcloth with her. Once my room door closes, I pray it's locked for tonight.

I tiptoe across the floor, and when I reach the brass handle and push it down, the door opens.

The irony.

Grabbing a chair, I push it under the handle door to give myself an illusion of safety. That's all it is, an illusion.

***

I wake up with pain bouncing against the inside of my skull. My hand trembles as I run my fingers across the lumps on the side of my head. If I thought Gilly was a nightmare, the proof that it happened lies under my fingertips. The chair is still propped against the door, and I scramble from the bed to remove it. I didn't want anyone questioning why I locked myself in my room. I get back into the bed; my gaze keeps dragging to the balcony doors. My mind skips and replays Gilly disappearing. I'm out of bed again as I tiptoe toward the door. I pull back the curtains, and the click of the lock opening has my heart lurching in my chest.

I step out onto the empty balcony. Looking over the edge, I can't understand how he got out safely. I check both sides, but there is no ladder or rope. I don't think he would leave a rope dangling. He clearly didn't jump, or I'd be looking at a body below me. A bird screeches in the sky, and I look up. The overhang above me catches my attention, and I push my back against the railing to try to see above me. It's another balcony.

Shivers race across my flesh. Is that Gilly's room? Is that how he gets in and out of my room? I'm scrambling back inside when the bedroom door opens.

Lily pauses and frowns. "Good morning." She tilts her head as she closes the door.

"Good morning," I respond, and that seems to squash the suspicious look in her eyes.

Lily helps me get dressed. She's not as chirpy as she normally is. She doesn't ask me what happened last night. Instead, she focuses on helping me get dressed for brunch with my family and some of Aidan's.

My gut clenches at the thought of seeing Gilly. "Is there a phone I can use?" I ask Lily. She pauses as she brushes my hair.

"Aidan said I could call my sister," I explain.

She smiles, but it doesn't reach her eyes. "Yes, Master Murphy told me. He said you can use the phone in his office."

His office? I would have access to his office. I drop my gaze as Lily finishes brushing my hair. The yellow summer dress is pretty. It's not a color I'd pick myself. I'm also surprised at the long sleeves and wonder yet again if Aidan knows why I cover my arms.

It doesn't matter. If my and my mother's plan works and Aidan kills my father, I could walk away from all this.

With that thought, I get up. I need to make sure Louise is safe.

Lily takes one more look at my face and seems happy with her work when she leads me from the room.

Aidan's office isn't what I expected. I pictured a small room, not an actual library. Books and more books line vast shelves. They call to me, though I can't imagine finding a Jane Austen among the antique reads.

I refocus on the slick black phone for a landline on Aidan's desk. I take a peek at Lily. She hasn't left me. Maybe that's a condition of Aidan's. I don't need to be alone. I just need to confirm that Louise is safe.

I pull out the leather chair and sit on the edge before dragging the chair close to the desk. It's an odd feeling sitting behind Aidan's desk. I wonder how many deals he's made while sitting here. What decisions were enforced from behind this desk? Did he issue orders to have men killed from here?

I pick up the phone to pull my mind away from the dark thoughts. The phone rings three times before Betty, the house manager, answers.

"Good morning, you have reached the Collins residence. Betty, house manager, speaking. How may I help?"

I smile at the sound of her voice. "Hi, Betty. It's Raven."

"Raven, how are you? We all miss you here." The fondness in Betty's tone isn't lost on me. I've always been her favorite.

"I miss you too," I say truthfully before peeking up at Lily, who gives me an encouraging smile. "Can I speak to Louise?"

"Most certainly. I'll put you through to her room. Take care, Raven," Betty finishes.

"I will." The line redirects and starts to ring. I glance at Aidan's laptop, which is in the darkness. What kind of information would I see if I powered it up? Would he have a password? There are no files or documents on the desk. The line continues to ring, and a heaviness has me gripping the phone tighter.

When the line picks up, I briefly close my eyes in relief. "Louise?"

"I'm sorry, Raven." Betty sounds troubled. "No one is picking up."

My lids snap open. "Can you please go check on her, Betty?"

"I've already sent Mike. Give me a moment."

My heart races and when I look at Lily, she steps closer to the desk. "We must go. Your parents are waiting." She sounds apologetic, but they can wait. I need to know that Louise is safe first.

The line rattles for a moment. It sounds as if Betty shifts the phone from one hand to another. I can make out muffled voices, but not exactly what they are saying. I rise, no longer able to sit still.

"Raven." Betty's voice is strained. "We can't find her."

My chest rises and falls as I think the worst. Gilly threatened me with getting to Louise, and now he has made good on that.

CHAPTER SEVENTEEN

Aidan

"I HEAR YOU WON big at the poker tables last night," Jason says to Raven's father. He's sporting a pair of bloodshot eyes and a weary smile this morning. So he fucking should. I can't bear to be in the man's presence. Yet here I am, doing my part for Frank, who didn't give me a moment of his time last night. I still have no answers as to why he thinks Gilly is fit to rule over us. I need to inform him about the O'Reagans not being impressed. He needs to know what he's causing among other Mafia groups.

"I did," Raven's father confirms as he leans forward and picks up a glass of champagne. It's early, too early for drinking, but that doesn't deter Raven's father from having his fill.

"Then you lost it all again," Raven's mother brazenly informs us as she smiles sweetly over the rim of her china cup. Her husband bristles and if we weren't present, I'm sure he would launch his drink right into her face. He could do it with us all sitting here, but he clearly is unsure how to act after last night. It's also clear that Raven's mother has grown a backbone overnight. And now I wonder why.

It's unusually hot for this time of the morning, and I'm tempted to pull open my jacket, but I remain still. Alex and Jason don't seem uncomfortable in their suits. I'm not sure if it's a charade, but I don't feel any level of comfort with this situation.

"Have a biscuit, darling." Raven's father speaks from the corner of his mouth to his wife. Fear flashes through her eyes, and it's the woman I saw at the table last night, the woman who's terrified of her husband.

I glance at the open doors that lead back into the house. Where is Raven? Once she gets here, we can all chat and pretend this is normal, and then my duty for today is done.

"You have such beautiful gardens." Raven's mother smiles at me. It's strained, forced, and begging for me to save her from her abusive husband.

"Thank you." I rise, done with this conversation. "I will go see what's keeping Raven."

"I'm sure she wants attention." Her father speaks out of turn.

He sinks further into the chair as I glare at him. I have never felt so fucking protective of anyone before. I loosen my tightening fists I don't remember clenching.

Alex wears a smirk, clearly spotting my reaction to the insult. I have to walk away. Hurting Gerry won't do me any favors. Once again, I hate the power that Raven holds over me. She isn't even here, and yet because of her, violence pumps and pulses through my system.

I enter the house and pick up the housekeeping phone. After three rings, Rose answers.

"Have you seen Raven?" I ask, while trying to keep my irritation at bay.

"Lily took her to your office to call her sister, Master Aidan."

"Thank you, Rose." I hang up and make my way to my office. The thought of her in such a personal space should annoy me, but it doesn't. I like the picture I create of Raven sitting behind my desk using my phone. Some of my anger shreds as I focus on that image. I reach the office but don't enter, as Raven's pitched voice makes me pause.

"Oh, God. She's missing." Fear fills Raven's words.

"Miss Raven. I'm sure she is fine."

Lily's soothing tone doesn't help. "You don't know that. You don't know what these people are capable of. They are monsters."

I've heard enough. I push open the door, and both Lily and Raven face me. Lily curtsies and has the respect to look horrified at Raven's accusation. She isn't wrong, but I don't like her spreading fear to my staff.

"Monsters?" I take her in from the tip of her cream shoes all the way past the yellow sundress covering every inch of her. Her dark hair hangs down her back, and once again, I hate how striking she is. Her nostrils flare as she reels in some of the hysteria. She doesn't look at all horrified at being caught speaking ill about me. Instead, she makes quick, light steps until she's standing in front of me.

"I need to speak to my mother." She sounds breathless, and an alarm bell goes off in my head.

"Is something wrong?" I ask, but my gaze snaps to Lily, who's watching us intently.

"You can leave us," I remark before I glance back at Raven.

Her blue eyes widen, and she blinks several times. Lily moves past us and curtsies while rushing from the room.

The moment we are alone, I can't stop myself as I reach out and rest my hand on her shoulder. Raven stiffens under my fingers, and it's enough to make me remove my hand.

"Nothing is wrong." She looks away from me. "I just need to speak to my mother."

She won't look at me, but I can't look away from her. Her tongue flicks out and moistens her lips, lips I want to kiss. I take a step toward her again. Her whole body grows tense as I reach out and take her cheek in my hand. "You can tell me if something is wrong."

Wide blue eyes stare up at me and, fuck, she's stunning. My cock grows hard as her lips part. She's considering something. Her eyes sparkle with gathering tears, and my worry for her deepens. She blinks and her lids flutter closed, cutting me off.

"I'm fine." She steps out of my touch.

I clench my jaw at the blatant rejection, but I refuse to let her see it. "Your mother is waiting with your father and my brothers. I know women like to be fashionably late, but I think you've taken it too far." I smirk at her before losing the smile and exhaling like she's on my last nerve. Which is actually the truth.

"Please. I would like to speak to my mother just for a moment." Her voice is small, and I shouldn't give in to her request. I should say no.

So why am I leaving my office? Lily lingers close to the door and snaps to attention when she sees me.

"Go get Raven's mother," I order her. Was she listening in?

She curtsies and scurries past. I watch her until she disappears. I'm tempted to go back into my office, but being around Raven leaves me conflicted. I take out my phone, which hasn't stopped buzzing, and see two missed calls from Gilly. I push the phone back into my pocket. I am in no mood for his gloating. When I look up, Raven's mother stands in front of me with Lily. She appears nervous.

"What's the matter?" She swallows. Her nervousness doesn't seem reasonable, but I'm getting sick of trying to figure out the Collins women.

"Raven is in the office. She wants a word. I'll be in the garden when you are both ready." I offer a smile, and she relaxes before heading into the office. Lily still stands in the hallway as Raven's mother closes the office door. Lily becomes aware that I'm watching her and she finally leaves.

I placed her to take care of Raven; maybe she is concerned what will happen to Raven if she's left alone with me. Her worry is fair. I have no idea what would happen if I was left long enough in Raven's company. I'm about to leave and keep good to my word about waiting outside, when Raven's voice catches my attention.

She's fretting about her sister being missing. Her mother tells her to calm down. Raven snaps back, telling her she won't.

"She's with my sister," the mother admits. "I couldn't tell you. But I sent her there for a while."

"Why?" Raven doesn't sound relieved. "Betty said she was in her room."

"I told Betty to lie. I had to."

"What aren't you telling me?" Raven's voice lowers.

"I was afraid of what would happen after you left."

Movement in the hall draws my attention to Alex. I don't want to leave the door, but he raises both brows.

"What happened?" Raven's voice rises again.

"Nothing, Raven. But the last time, it got ugly."

Silence fills the room, and I want to tell Alex to fuck off, but he's still standing and waiting. I walk to my brother and offer him a pat on the arm. "What is it?"

"Your guests are getting impatient."

"The only one I give a fuck about isn't out there." I release Alex's arm.

His gaze narrows, and he lifts his chin up. "You care for her?"

My gut twists. "Am I not meant to? You did, after all, vote for me to marry her."

Alex doesn't answer me, but his brows drag down.

"No, I don't care for her," I answer.

The look Alex gives me tells me he isn't convinced. That pisses me off. What the fuck has it got to do with him if I care for her or not?

"I'll let your guests know you're coming soon," Alex says and leaves me feeling troubled.

I return to the door, ready to knock, but Raven and her mother are still deep in conversation. They must think the room is soundproof.

Raven's mother's voice rises this time. "You need to make him hit you. You agreed to this last night."

I'm wondering if she wants me to hit her. My jaw clenches. That would never happen. I might be a lot of things, but I don't abuse women.

"Then what, Mother? You really want us to be responsible for his death?"

I'm ready to laugh; they think they can kill me. How entertaining.

"Aidan won't kill him. He'll just protect you by maybe taking his hand first." The mother sounds delighted, and it all clicks into place.

"You have no idea what you're asking me. I saw him cut off a man's finger." Raven speaks like she's talking about a monster. I hate how she sees me.

"We'd better go. They will be wondering what's taking us so long."

I walk back outside and the heat hits me smack in the face. This time, I unbutton the top two buttons of my shirt.

I'm seated with a glass of ice-cold water in my hand when Raven and her mother arrive. They both smile.

"I apologize for the delay. I was talking to my sister and..." She raises one shoulder. Alex and Jason rise as do I. Jason is the closest to Raven, and he is the first to press a kiss to her cheek. It shouldn't annoy me, but it does.

"You don't have to apologize," Alex says as he takes Raven's hand and presses a kiss to it.

She gives a shaky smile, and when she looks at me, the small smile vanishes. She thinks I'm a fucking monster. I can see the fear flash in her eyes. I don't give her a moment but step closer and wrap a hand around the back of her neck. She tries to pull away, but I don't allow it as I press my lips against hers. It takes only a second before she relaxes into the kiss, but it's a second too late. I break the kiss and release her. She glances at her mother, who's sitting back down on the wicker couch, and that's where Raven joins her. Her father hasn't acknowledged her arrival. He's too busy gulping down his champagne. Rose has arrived with fresh tea and light biscuits, and Raven's father leans into her, waving his empty glass to be refilled.

Rose takes the glass, but he doesn't release it. "Just bring the bottle," he snarls. When Rose leaves, his gaze meets mine. I want to ram the glass down his fucking throat.

Yet, I'm sitting here sipping iced water as if I'm a gentleman and not a fucking monster.

"Louise didn't seem sick at all." Raven speaks to her father, and I wonder if she's putting her plan of making her father hit her into motion.

Her father looks at her from the corner of his eye. "That's great." He doesn't give two fucks. All he cares about is the bottle of champagne placed in front of him. He fills his glass to the top, and when he raises it, the liquid sloshes across his fingers.

Raven's face heats as she watches her father's gluttony.

"I know I've said it before, but your home is truly exquisite." Raven's mother layers on the compliments. I see her differently now, whispering in her daughter's ear. Has she thought for one second what might happen if her husband loses his control, which is very likely, and I don't intervene? I mean, I don't have to. I know I will, but I don't have to. That's the part that bothers me.

"Thank you. One day I may visit your home," I say.

She seems taken aback. "That would be... lovely." She glances at Raven, but Raven focuses on the cup in her hand.

"Alex, is it?" Raven's mother says with a smile. "What do you do?"

"Celine, can you shut the fuck up?" Raven's father barks.

"She can ask a question, Gerry." Alex leans forward. He wears a relaxed smile, but I know Raven's father is rustling his feathers. None of us like a man who speaks down to a woman. It's not how we were raised.

"Don't speak to her like that." I might admire Raven's bravery if I didn't know the truth behind her actions. She's using this moment to force her father's hand.

I need to stop this before that happens, yet I'm sitting back in the chair. Jason lights up a cigar, like watching this doesn't bother him. It does. It bothers us all.

Raven's father's jaw tightens, and he reaches for the bottle and refills his glass.

"Would you like a bucket?" Raven says smartly. He turns with such force that his drink spills across his hand. I'm moving before I can think. I'm beside him, bearing down on him. The gun is heavy under my jacket, and I'm doing everything not to extract the weapon.

Gerry wisely sits back in his seat and sips his champagne. "A bucket sounds great." He smiles.

I haven't moved and know everyone watches me. I look at Raven's mother. Her eyes shine. She knows she's right. If he lays a hand on Raven, I'll kill him and now I've proven her point. A point I had intended not to prove.

I move away from Raven's father and hold out my hand to Raven. She stiffens, her eyes wide, but she places her cup on the saucer.

"This was lovely, but I think Raven and I will take a walk." I don't look at anyone as I speak. I can't stay here and keep watching Raven provoke her father. She must think I'm a dog that will bite someone who gets too close to her. The angry part of me hates that she's right. But I also refuse to be part of her ruse.

Her small hand slips into mine.

"Enjoy your walk." Raven's mother's voice wobbles. She will be alone with her husband. Raven hesitates, but I tighten my hold on her. I don't give a rat's ass what her mother faces and neither should Raven, yet she isn't moving. She pulls her hand out of mine, and in front of everyone, stares up at me.

"I think I'll stay here," she voices.

In her mind, I'm not just a dog who will bite for her; she also thinks I will bark, too. She's very fucking wrong.

CHAPTER EIGHTEEN

RAVEN

NAUSEA BURNS THE BACK of my throat. I have no other words for what's happening right now. Aidan smiles at me, but there's nothing nice about the way his lips twist.

"We're going for a walk. Right now, Raven." His words are low and clipped, yet everyone is in earshot to hear his command. That is exactly what it is, a command.

I want to tell him no. I'm so sick and tired of everyone telling me what to do. The memory of Gilly in my room, threatening my sister, forcing me to... I have to push the image away, or I will throw up. I give in and nod at Aidan.

He doesn't look like a man who just won. He looks like a man who's ready to snap. As I step around the table, I keep my gaze diverted from my mother. I can't bear to see that look of panic I'm sure will shine in her gaze as I leave her with my father.

"I will be departing, too. Unfortunately, work calls." Alex rises, and he takes my hand and places a kiss to the back of it.

He pats Aidan on the shoulder, who stands directly behind me. The day is hot enough, but with Aidan towering against my back, I may as well be stuck in a sauna.

I stupidly glance up at Aidan, and no matter how hot the weather is, it doesn't scare off the cold that settles around my heart from the anger his dark eyes reveal.

He starts to walk, and I obediently fall into step beside him. Once we leave the comfort of the awning, there is nothing to stop the sun beating down on us. It takes a moment before Aidan removes his navy suit jacket. My heart triples in speed as the heavy silver gun he wears becomes visible. He's carrying a gun. An actual gun. My heart continues to slam into my chest. I run my hands along the sides of my yellow sundress to try to calm my frazzled nerves.

"Did you have a good chat with your sister?" he asks. I'm not sure if he's aware of how clenched his jaw is.

"Yes." I focus on the gardens that sprawl around us. We're getting close to the sheds, and they remind me of when Aidan said a man inside had betrayed him.

"No," I insert abruptly, not wanting to find myself inside one of the sheds.

"Which is it, Raven, yes or no?"

I glance at Aidan, he's watching me. His obsidian eyes send shivers snaking and curling around the base of my spine.

I'm thinking as fast as I can. Telling him my sister is with my aunt won't do any harm. It's not like he would share the information with my father. Lying to him right now just doesn't seem wise.

"She wasn't there. I never got to speak to her."

Aidan stops walking, forcing me to stop, too. I'm ready to run my hands along the side of my dress when Aidan's gaze narrows. I flex my fingers like a cat stretching to stop myself from doing what I really want.

"She's with my auntie. It's the safest place she could be." I'm not just thinking about how dangerous my father is; I'm also thinking about Gilly. My nerves are a jumbled mess.

"Safe from what?" Aidan asks, and his words pull my head out of a dark cloud of fear.

I shrug. My mother said the last time things got ugly. What happened to my sister? If something had happened, wouldn't she have told me? My fingers tighten around the fabric of my dress. It's then I realize I've been running my hands along my sides again.

"I don't know," I answer, stopping the rubbing by folding my arms across my chest.

Aidan isn't moving; instead, he steps closer, the gun becoming closer, and I drop my hands.

"Why did you lie? Why pretend you spoke to your sister?" His questions lead to more questions.

I'm ready to reach for the sides of my dress, but I pause as Aidan's gaze flickers to my hands.

I don't answer, and he grins before he starts to walk again. It takes me a moment to pull myself together before I follow him.

We walk until the manicured lawns grow a little wilder and the trees become thicker, offering some shade from the overbearing sun.

I take in Aidan's wide shoulders, and he scares me for more than one reason. Being next to him stirs up emotions I shouldn't feel. When Gilly had mentioned me being his wife, the loss I felt at losing Aidan didn't make sense. Gilly said I was too much trouble, and I had no idea what that meant. My mind skips forward, like someone hitting fast forward before the image in my head slows down to the point he's forcing me to touch him. I fold my arms again and focus on Aidan's shoulders, which shift under his pristine white shirt.

I try to gather all the knowledge I have now. My sister is safe. My father doesn't even know where she is. He thinks she's at home, so that gives my mind some rest. I need to figure out a way to protect myself. Aidan glances at me over his shoulder, his gaze sharp and not as angry as it was before.

My heart triples in speed as a plan forms very quickly in my head. Aidan would protect me from Gilly. Staying in my room is too dangerous. There is nothing stopping Gilly from continuing to abuse me.

I swallow and try to calm my nerves. "The party for our engagement went well."

When I start to speak, Aidan completely stops walking. When he turns, I want to shut up. I want his attention, yet I don't. He's formidable, a vortex of everything masculine. I have no warning when he steps toward me. My feet move on their own accord to step me back.

He hasn't said anything, and I'm not ready to duck and cover yet. "I think we should stay in the same room." He takes another step toward me while brushing some hair out of his eye. Why is that so sexy? What is wrong with me? I take another step back. "I mean, we would sleep on different sides of the bed, but sharing a room with all the staff watching us could be wise."

He takes another step, and when I step back, hard bark digs into my spine. The shade from the tree doesn't help with the heat that heightens and burns every single piece of my covered flesh.

I can't hold his gaze, so I focus instead on the daisies at my feet. I start to count them, but when his shoes appear in my line of sight, I swallow. "I don't mind sleeping on the floor," I whisper.

Anything but staying in my room. Anything? Would I go further with Aidan in order to have his protection?

"You want to sleep in my bed?" His voice is deep, gravely, and it rolls across my flesh, raising every hair in its wake.

My breaths are shaky as I count five daisies and run my hands along my sides before I force myself to remain calm. "Yes." I look up, and what a bad decision that is.

His dark eyes are devoid of anything, only darkness can be seen there. He moves until our chests touch, and it's too much. I reach up and place my hand to push him away. The moment the tips of my fingers touch the soft fabric of his shirt, he reacts. Like flint being struck by a match. His hands are in my hair, his mouth lands on mine. I'm caught up in a storm that's frantic, and I know if I want to jump, I need to do it now before I'm devoured. His warm lips and wet mouth along with the scent of his cologne have my fingers balling into a fist, and I'm dragging him closer.

His large fingers probe my scalp before they tighten around the dark locks, and the burn of my head has me groaning. The noise gets swallowed up as Aidan slips his tongue into my mouth.

I can't think.

I can't cope.

I can't stop this.

Heat spreads through my body, and dampness has me tightening my thighs together. Every cell in my body throbs with need. I can't stop the onslaught of excitement and the adrenaline that demands I keep going. Even if I wanted to stop, I don't think I can.

Aidan's hand leaves my hair and trails along my neck. There is nothing gentle about his touch; I feel it down to my toes. My tongue dances with his, and when he presses closer, his erection pushes against my stomach. The heaviness should be my wake-up call, but it's not.

The sound of footsteps has me coming up for air. Even after Aidan breaks the kiss, the spell he's cast over me doesn't disappear. He's holding my neck, his breaths blowing across my lips in fast succession as his gaze devours me even more so than the kiss. My knees grow weak. My heart beats wildly.

Someone clears their throat, and I want to turn and see who it is, but Aidan keeps me pinned where we are.

"Gilly and Frank have arrived and would like to see you," Jason says from the other side of the tree.

"I'll be there in a moment," Aidan replies, and his fingers slip from my neck and hair. He doesn't step away, and I listen to Jason's footsteps as they grow more distant.

Gilly is here. Would he try something in daylight? Would Aidan send me to my room and give Gilly an opening to hurt me? He hadn't said he would agree to me sharing a room with him. I drop my gaze, and Aidan finally steps away from me. He picks up his jacket from the ground. I hadn't even noticed he dropped it. When he's standing again, I walk toward him. He doesn't speak and neither do I. That didn't go as I expected. The kiss was unexpected. My tongue flicks out, and I lick my lips. I can still taste him in my mouth. The closer we get to the house, the clearer the view of the people becomes.

My mother and father are still seated. My father leans toward Gilly, animated with his words. My stomach roils and my footing slows, noticeably forcing Aidan to stop.

"Are you okay?" He holds out a hand to me as if I should take it.

I don't. I find my footing again. "I'm just very warm."

Gilly and Frank both cease their conversation and look at Aidan and me. I'm waiting for Aidan to dismiss me, and I'm ready to go back into the house. I can't look at Gilly. I'm afraid of what I might see. I can't look at Jason after what he might have seen. I can't look at my mother, as guilt from leaving her with my father gnaws in my stomach. I can't look at my father, so I look at Frank and find him watching me.

"Raven, you look so beautiful. My nephew is a lucky man." He breaks the distance and presses a kiss to both my cheeks. "You've met my son?" Without a moment of respite, he's turning me toward Gilly, whom I have no choice but to look at.

"Yes, I have."

Gilly smiles sweetly at me. He doesn't appear angry like I expected, and I think that's a bit more terrifying. "Lovely to see you again, Raven."

Last night flashes through my mind, and without thought, I reach out and find myself grabbing for Aidan's hand. When his large fingers encase my hand, I realize what I've done. Glancing up at Aidan, I'm expecting to see a surprised or suspicious look in his eyes. Instead, he isn't focused on me.

"Rose, could you have Raven's belongings taken to my room?"

The space spins. He's letting me stay with him. I'm conflicted, even more so after that kiss. Lying beside Aidan Murphy won't be easy.

"Raven, Raven, you are delightful." The high-pitched female voice is from Frank's wife, Isabella. She steps out of the house and toward me with outstretched arms. Her fingers and wrists drip with gold, while the rest of her is wrapped in white cotton trousers and a top. She's a picture of wealth with her sun-kissed skin and soft blonde hair. She pulls me into a hug. "Stunning. You are a breath of fresh air."

Her compliments heat my skin. "Thank you."

She leans out but doesn't release me. Aidan hasn't released my hand either, and my body overheats now.

"It's so warm out here." She releases me as she glances around at everyone.

Frank has seated himself across from my father. Gilly stands close to my mother, and I don't look at either of them. My gaze skims Jason, who's watching me and Aidan.

"It's very warm. We will go for a swim and cool down." Before I can answer, she turns to my mother. "All the ladies."

My mother rises, and it's the first time I look at her. "That sounds great." She's nodding enthusiastically, but the hysteria in her movements tells me that after I departed, things didn't go smoothly. Did my father hurt her? I scan her body from head to toe, but I don't see any marks.

"Fantastic." Isabella smiles at me. "We shall let the men talk."

Fear has me releasing Aidan's hand. "I'm fine. But thank you." I keep my hands at my side.

"I insist," Isabella says.

My mother reaches me and links her arm through mine like we're best friends. "Of course we will, Isabella. The offer is so kind."

I don't want to.

"We will let the men talk," Isabella repeats before she winks at me, and I'm being pulled toward the house. I take a final look behind me, only to find Aidan staring. I have no idea what he's thinking, but I'm inside, in the shade, and that counts for something. I'll take anything but being in Gilly's presence.

"I will meet you at the pool. My room is this way." Isabella points down the hall.

"Mine too," my mother chirps, and I don't want to be alone. But I'm released as they start walking down the hall. Isabella glances at me over her shoulder and gives me a smile.

I walk to the stairs, and I'm hyperaware of every noise. Gilly wouldn't follow me in daylight, would he?

I'm taking the stairs two at a time and stop running when I reach the landing. A security man is stationed outside my room. I take solace in his appearance.

"I don't want anyone to come into my room. No matter what," I order.

He nods. "Of course, Miss Collins."

I enter my room, and the first thing I do is lock the balcony doors before the reality that I have to get into a bathing suit slams into me. This is a disaster.

I close my eyes and take a few steadying breaths. Isabella and my mother will be the only ones who see me. The men are outside, I reason with the panic that pounds my system. I can wear a pool wrap up and down the hallway. Under the water, maybe no one will notice the scars on my arms.

My stomach twists painfully as I enter my wardrobe and take down the red one-piece swimsuit. It's simple, but of course, there are no sleeves.

I kick off my shoes as dread devours my courage. I can only pray that Isabella doesn't pay too much attention to my arms.

I strip off the yellow dress. I don't want to take long. I don't like being up here alone. I just hope the security man keeps his word.

I quickly pull on the red bathing suit and stand in front of the full-length mirror. I feel sick as I take in my appearance. I'm not sure how long I'm standing here staring at the scars that nearly destroyed me. Each one holds a nightmare.

My gaze snags on the handle. Is it moving? The door starts to open and my gaze collides with dark eyes. They are as dark as a starless night, and they slowly take me in.

CHAPTER NINETEEN

AIDAN

RAVEN HAD ONLY LEFT when I wanted to follow her. I need to know why she reached out and took my hand earlier. There was something in how her body reacted to Gilly that set me off. I can't be sure, but my instincts are usually right.

I excuse myself and enter the house. Lily and Rose are busy in the kitchen, which means Raven is alone. The idea delights me as I climb the stairs.

"Miss Collins has requested no one enter." Thomas relays the message that Raven must have given him.

I smirk, liking how she used the security I have provided her, and which she should. I nod at him. But no matter what instructions Raven relays to my staff, I am their primary master. So the rules don't apply to me. I turn the handle. I should knock, but this is my home. The moment I push open the door, I know I should leave, but I don't.

I walk in and close the door behind me. Raven spins, her eyes wide, like she can't believe I'm standing in her room. Her long legs are perfect; her chest fills the swimsuit perfectly. She's flawless. I'm taking a step closer as I zero in on the scars along her arms. Fire flares to life in my gut, and I have to stop walking as it turns into an inferno.

"What happened?" My voice is low, and I think there is no way she heard my question.

Her blue eyes dart to the bed, where a dressing gown lies. She's ready to bolt, and I should let her.

I move quickly and grab her wrist, forcing her to stay put. Her pulse beats frantically under the tips of my fingers. Her cheeks are red, and her breasts rise up and fall at a fast pace.

Even as fury fuels my every thought at the marks on her arms, my cock starts to grow from standing this close to her. She smells of something citric, like oranges.

Raven wraps her free arm around her waist like she can cover herself up. "I had an accident."

My fingers tighten, and when she bites her bottom lip, I loosen my hold. "Don't lie to me." I need to know what happened to her. Raven finally looks at me. It's the first time I've ever seen such deadness in her eyes.

"I was in a car accident." She holds my gaze, and I can't decipher a lie. I glance down at the scars, wanting to remove every one of them. When I had her clothes ordered, her mother had given me measurements and also made the request that her dresses and tops have long sleeves. I hadn't questioned the request. I didn't care at the time. But now I can see why.

My fingers move across the ridged scars. Raven inhales a sharp breath at the contact and doesn't release it. I have this overwhelming urge to kiss each silvery imperfection. I'm back, looking at Raven's face. Her eyes are closed, and a tear makes a pathway down her cheek. I can't help but wonder who she is. What is the essence of Raven? I release her wrist and take her face in my hand. Her lids flutter open, and her gaze pools with so much pain. Pain I recognize.

"Did it hurt?" I find myself asking. Of course it fucking hurt. What kind of stupid fucking question am I asking her?

She blinks and more tears spill. "Severely." She folds and allows me to see the pain shine in her eyes. I want to run from her; I need to find a shade that will stop her from burning me. That's what she's doing, burning away every rational thought I have. She's dangerous. I shouldn't be here. I shouldn't be so focused on her.

But she's consuming my every thought and decision.

My gaze dips lower to her full chest before I look back up into her eyes. Her pain is more concealed now.

"What happened?"

She sniffles and blinks rapidly. "What do you mean?"

My fingers run along the back of her neck as I grip her and move her closer. "The car accident? What happened?"

Her head pushes against my hand like she's trying to get away. She reaches up to fold her arms, but there isn't much room. Her fingers brush my chest and my body reacts like it shouldn't.

She shrugs. "I mean, it was two cars." She won't look at me. "It happened so quickly."

"How long ago?" I ask.

"One year." Her answer is quick, and she glances up at me. Pain twists her features.

"I'm sorry, Raven."

My apology seems to shock her, but it has me releasing her neck. "I'll let you finish getting ready." She's in too much pain, and all I want to do right now is devour her.

"I don't want Isabella to see me like this." Raven turns and walks to the bed. I get the full view of her peachy rear. Jesus, she's perfection. All that flesh disappears under the pool wrap. And when she turns to me, she tightens the robe. "I'd prefer not to go swimming."

I nod, agreeing. I don't want anyone to see her. "I think that's wise."

She flinches like I've struck her. She grips the belt of the robe like it's a lifeline.

"Was the other driver drinking?" I need to know more. When will I learn just to leave?

"I don't want to talk about it," Raven snaps. Her cheeks turn red, her gaze downcast. Her change in attitude makes me walk to her.

"A month ago, my father took his life." My confession doesn't just shock Raven but sends waves skittering through me.

"I'm so sorry." She covers her mouth, her early attitude dispelled. Just like I wanted. So I can leave now.

"He hung himself," I admit.

Raven sucks in a large lungful of air. "That's terrible."

I grin, but it freezes on my face. "He put a rope around his neck, stood up on a step stool, and jumped. I often wonder at what point he thought he couldn't do this to his sons. That he couldn't leave us swimming in my shit."

Raven reaches out, and I step away from her touch. I'm glad she tried to comfort me, because it's a wake-up call to how weak I must sound.

"He was weak," I quickly say, stuffing my hands into my pockets.

Raven is shaking her head. "No, Aidan. That's not a weakness."

What does she know about my life? About what makes my father weak or not. "You should get dressed. I don't want you swimming. Cover yourself up," I bark before I turn and leave the room.

I can't bear to think of anyone seeing Raven in a tiny swimsuit. She's mine, and I refuse to have other men ogle her.

I make my way downstairs and stop at the front reception room, where Gilly speaks into Lily's ear and whispers something. She giggles as he leans away. Her cheeks are red with excitement, her gaze glazed over with awe.

"What are you doing?" I ask as I walk toward them.

Gilly's smile vanishes along with Lily's. Is that contempt I see in her eyes?

"Have you no work to do?" I ask.

Her gaze snaps to Gilly, who has the gall to roll his eyes. "Where did you leave your whip, Aidan? Can't she have a five-minute break?"

I smirk. I don't give two fucks who Gilly is riding. Just not my fucking staff. "Has something happened between you and Raven? I ask because she seemed... uneasy," I settle on, but that doesn't seem right.

Gilly shrugs, but I notice how Lily stiffens. She still hasn't left, and I'm ready to tell her to leave when Gilly speaks.

"I might have paid her a few compliments. I think she might be attracted to me. No one could blame her." He smirks again and winks at Lily, who basks in his attention.

I can't move. If I do, I'll fucking kill him. "I highly doubt you could attract the likes of Raven Collins." At that, I glance at Lily to let him know I know who he's fucking.

His smile melts off his face, and he brazenly walks up to me like this is some challenge. "If I wanted her, I could have her like that." He clicks his fingers, emphasizing his words.

I reach out and grip the two fingers, then I bend them back. His screams are like a lullaby to a baby—that's how much I soak up his pain. I want to rip them from his fucking hand.

"Let my son go." Frank's voice doesn't have me releasing Gilly, who's bent at the knees in pain. I push further and know they will snap easily. He roars.

"Now." Frank's voice booms.

It takes more self-control than I thought I possessed to release Gilly's fingers. He grabs his hand, his face red as he looks around the room.

"He's a fucking psycho." He's screaming past me to his father.

I smile at him, wishing to God that he retaliated. A bullet would be too good for Gilly.

"Then why provoke him?" Frank snaps as he stands beside me like we are a united front, which is total horseshit.

Gilly's face darkens. "He can't put his hands on me," Gilly roars as he cradles his hand to his chest. He takes a look at Lily, who's watching our exchange. When her gaze meets mine, she focuses on the floor.

"You," Frank snaps at her, and I don't appreciate him speaking to my staff. "Get out." His anger isn't justified, and I wonder if he knows his prodigal son is fucking my staff.

Lily scurries from the room, and Gilly glares at his father. He's more controlled now and lets his hand drop to his side, but I notice how stiffly he holds his two fingers.

"He needs to be punished. I'll think of something fitting." Gilly holds his head high, and I focus on his neck and how I'd like to snap it. I push my hands into my trousers pockets to stop myself from giving in to my creative thoughts.

"Give us a minute." Frank speaks before walking past Gilly.

"What..."

"Now, Gilbert." Frank's voice raises an octave.

I grin at Gilly, and he pauses before passing me. "This isn't over." He shoulders me.

"You got that fucking right," I fire back as he leaves the room, giving me the time I also want with Frank.

"So, that is the leader of our family," I say. He's Frank's son, but he knows that Gilly isn't fit to lead a group of preschoolers across a fucking road, never mind the most deadly men in Ireland. Frank doesn't answer me. "I have great faith in the future of the Irish Mafia." I continue to let my sarcasm about the situation leave my lips. "I'm sure Shay O'Reagan is opening a bottle of champagne right about now."

Frank finally looks at me, firing a warning for me not to continue with my outburst.

"Shay O'Reagan cut a man's head off," I tell him. "He is also very much against Gilly's leading."

"I know," Frank admits.

This makes no sense. "Richard O'Reagan spent time in a madhouse. He is also against Gilly's leadership. That's the people who actually spoke to me."

"I'm very much aware of what the O'Reagans think." Frank folds his arms.

I pull my hands out of my pockets. "Then why?" I ask, raising them in the air. "Why make him the next to rule?"

Frank is fighting with some kind of internal battle. He can't bail on me. I need to fucking know what's going on.

I drop my hands. "Frank!" I prompt.

"I didn't," he finally gives in. He exhales. "I didn't make Gilly the next in line to rule."

He runs his hand across his mouth like I'd seen him do a million times when he had a beard. "I made a deal with the Bratva. So, in return, they have requested some favors." Frank says the word like it leaves a bad taste in his mouth.

The door opens and Jason walks in. He pauses. "Am I interrupting something?"

I fold my arms across my chest. Frank looks so small and weak right now. This is who's making decisions for me and my brothers' futures.

"Not at all. Frank is just informing me that the Bratva have their hands up his arse and are making his decision for him."

The door clicks softly behind Jason.

Frank rushes toward me. I expect his reaction, and when he grabs me by the neck, I don't act.

"Watch your fucking tongue. This changes nothing."

This changes everything. I grit my jaw to keep the words in.

"Aidan didn't mean any disrespect. It's a lot to take in," Jason says calmly, and that calm finds its way to Frank, who releases me.

"You knew." I speak to Jason while rubbing my neck.

He nods in response, but his gaze holds no guilt.

"Is there anything else I should know? Any other bargains you made with the Bratva?" I ask. Frank said they had requested favors.

Making Gilly lead our people isn't a favor. It's setting us up to fall. How could Frank let this happen? My father wouldn't have. We can't let this stand.

"Raven's father is bankrupt. You marrying her doesn't enhance our family, as I told you."

I can't speak. I peek at Jason and can see from the shocked look on his face that this is news to him too.

"It was a request from the Bratva that she marry into our family."

"She has ties with the Bratva?" I speak through clenched teeth. "Why not just tell me this?" I'm fighting for control.

"I have no idea why the Bratva have asked this of me, but I couldn't say no. It was easier than explaining we are in debt to them."

This time, I snap and clear the space between me and Frank. He doesn't cower away from me. "Correction, you are in debt to the Bratva."

I'm so riled up that I quickly walk away before I do something that will get me killed. No matter what, Frank leads our family, and right now, I'm bordering on giving him a right to fucking shoot me for questioning him. I need to calm down.

"I'm not happy about this either, but the fact still remains. We are indebted to the Bratva," he says. I glance at him, and he's begging me to disagree.

"What did the Bratva do for you to garner all these favors?" It must be something of epic proportions to have this add up.

"They're going to hand us the East of Ireland." Frank smiles.

"That's O'Reagan territory," I say.

"Exactly. Imagine them out of the way."

I shake my head. "In theory, Frank, that would be great. But right now, the O'Reagans are walking around and firing off threats. Do you know they considered clipping Matty? The idea of Gilly ruling has them all riled up. So forgive me if I don't see the logic in all this."

Frank's smile widens. He steps up to me and places a hand on my shoulder. "We want them riled up, son."

I want to shrug his hand off my shoulder. I'm not his fucking son.

"When they're all angry and raging, we come in strategically and wipe them off the face of the earth."

He pats my shoulder. "And don't worry if it doesn't make sense. That's why I am leading and you aren't."

A kick in the fucking face. Frank releases me. He walks past, and I stay rooted to the spot.

"Tomorrow, the Bratva will be here. So, a small gathering for a meet and greet. They may call in a favor, which I expect you boys to fulfill."

"Of course, Frank," Jason answers.

I can't. I can't answer right now. The door closes and Jason lets out a heavy breath. "That went spectacularly."

He moves to the large ornate wooden globe and pulls open the top, revealing a range of bottles of spirits. He fills two glasses with brandy and walks to me before handing me a glass like we can drink to our destruction.

My fingers tighten around the glass, and Jason stands in front of me, raising his into the air. "To family."

I sneer. "That's what you call this?" I walk to the fireplace and place my glass on the mantelpiece before leaving the room. I'm storming through the house, seeking some kind of release from the anger that tears through me. If I stumble across Gilly, I might not be able to hold back.

It's not Gilly who I cross but Raven, her black hair soaked from her swim I told her not to go for. She raises her head.

"I told you not to go swimming," I say.

Isabella and her mother pause behind her. Their annoying chatter ceases.

"I changed my mind," Raven tries to defend her actions.

"I didn't change mine," I remind her.

She pales and when I glance at Isabella and her mother, both women wear a look of disappointment.

"You can't keep your monster hidden." Raven's comment pulls my attention away from the other women, and it confuses me as she dashes past.

That's one thing about me. I don't let people run from me. Raven will learn that soon, very soon. As I follow her up the stairs, anger propels me every step of the way.

CHAPTER TWENTY

RAVEN

I PUSH DOWN THE panic that rises like a tsunami threatening to crush me. "Don't walk away from me." Aidan's voice forces my shoulders to hunch forward, but I won't stop. I can't. Anger at his look of pure disgust pushes me forward. I know my scars are bad, but the way he told me not to go swimming and cover up, made me feel like I was Quasimodo.

I had paced my room, convincing myself of all the reasons I should stay out of sight. I mean, I didn't want to go swimming, but I've been shoved around by too many people. So, I made the decision to go against Aidan's will. Do I regret it? No. No, I don't.

"Raven." Aidan's voice drops along with the temperature in my room. My security man doesn't blink as I pass him. Earlier, I told him not to let anyone enter, and yet Aidan had been in my room. Logically, I know it's Aidan's home, and no one would be fit to stop him. But it doesn't remove the injustice that inserts itself into my gaze, which I narrow at my bodyguard.

I don't make it far into my room before Aidan's arm circles around my waist, and I'm dragged back into his chest. I try to see his face, but he restrains me by tucking me harder against him.

The room flickers in and out of focus. The duvet changes from the soft gray to a deep burgundy. I blink as my chest tightens.

"I told you not to go swimming. You disobeyed me," Aidan whispers.

My throat and eyes burn. The floor seems to shift under my bare feet. The room around me dissolves, and I'm standing in Victor's room. I try to see Aidan to calm my frantic mind and realize this isn't Victor who keeps me held tightly against him, but Aidan keeps me pinned as my reality continues to crash and collide with the nightmare I lived.

"Let me go." My voice is small, breathless.

"When I say you can't do something. I mean it." Aidan seems oblivious to my impending meltdown.

"Let me go," I say louder. I squeeze my eyes shut as the memory of Victor holding me like this has me bending forward. "Let me go!" I scream.

I'm dragged right back. "No." Aidan's words are cold, dark and fueled with hate.

Through a palpitating heart and a chest that threatens to cave, I find a sliver of calm that I cling to. It's fickle and fragile, and I'm trying not to tear it to shreds with my claws of pure black fear.

"What do you want, an apology? Fine. I'm sorry. I'm sorry I let them see how disfigured I am. I'm sorry I brought shame to you. I'm sorry they saw what I truly am." My lip trembles as I speak to the four-poster bed. "How's that?" I ask, reining in the pain. "That good enough for you?" I can only appreciate that the room no longer resembles Victor's.

Aidan's only response is, "You call that an apology?"

I crane my neck to try to see him, and he allows the action this time. His sneer sends a warning to my fragile mind. Exhaustion has me dropping my shoulders. Without Aidan holding me, I think I'd slump to the floor. I look away from him and focus on his hands, which are still wrapped around me. A small diamond-shaped scar on his thumb soaks up my focus.

"What happened to your hand?" I ask.

"You want to swap war stories?" he fires back while letting me go.

My body stiffens, and I lock my knees so I don't sink to the floor. That won't happen. I fold my arms across my chest as I turn to face Aidan.

He looks as exhausted as I feel. Aidan runs a hand through his hair before he speaks. "Jason stabbed me with a pen." There is no anger in his words; he actually sounds amused. "He was pissed." Aidan grins, and it's the first sign of human life after his explosive rage.

Why does that small action make me think of Louise? The dark edges around my vision soften. "What was he angry about?" I ask and slowly walk to the bed, where I sit. For just a moment, I want something like the tale of a brotherly row to consume me. Stabbing each other is excessive, but at least it was a pen.

"A girl." Aidan continues to smile. "Caroline. She had hair the color of wheat. Freckles across her nose and a smile that had us Murphys at her feet."

My stomach clenches at how he speaks about this Caroline. I don't delve into my internal turmoil. I can't bear to face the truth of this moment.

I'm jealous.

"Jason had staked his claim on her first and, of course, we all showed respect and let him." Aidan walks past the dressing table, and I catch his eye in the mirror. "I couldn't let her go. At eleven, I was madly in love."

"Eleven?" I ask with too much relief.

Aidan turns, and I fear he's heard the relief. "I asked her out, but she turned me down." Aidan raises his hands in the air before dropping them. "She told Jason that I had asked her out." He grins, and his eyes take on a different look, one I haven't seen. Is this Aidan relaxed and happy? I'd like to see more of it. I'm exhausted from fighting my fears. At times, I want to give into them. Scream at someone to do their worst so it's out of the way. I wrap my arms around me, fighting off the conflicting emotions that demand my attention. I don't want to entertain any of them. I want to become numb.

"So he stabbed you with a pen?" I ask. My voice doesn't sound like my own. Aidan must notice, as his smile vanishes and his gaze grows dark. It's the darkness I'm used to, but I'm sad to see it return.

"Let's talk about you for a moment."

I don't want to.

"I went swimming because..." I shrug.

Aidan shakes his head. "Not about that. I will address your disobeying me later, but I want to know about the Bratva."

Aidan may as well have hit me square in the chest with a hammer. The air is vacuumed from the room. My mind scurries for a dark corner to hide in, but there is none. Aidan moves closer. My fingers trail to my arms, which I grip like I can push the memory away of every time Victor hurt me. My nails dig through the robe and into my arms. It lends me a moment to take air into my lungs. Aidan's gaze lands on my tightened fingers, and I loosen my hold, but it's too late.

"Were you really in a car accident?"

My body betrays me as it trembles. My voice is hidden, and all I can do is nod.

"You're lying," Aidan says gently. There's no anger in his words as he stops and kneels down at my feet like I'm his queen. I can't explain it, but as he looks up at me, I hang on for dear life so I don't break with him at my feet.

"You're terrified. I can see it in your eyes." He reaches up, and when his fingers touch my cheek, I'm so close to caving that it's frightening.

"The Bratva are the ones who hurt you?" He's asking, telling.

Air evaporates again, and I don't shake my head like I should. I part my lips, not to answer but to suck in small sips of precious air.

"Let me help you." Aidan's words are so sincere I want to reach out and accept his help. It would be so nice to have someone to share this with. Would he help me? Or is Gilly right, that he would kill me and Victor? That thought is sobering.

When I continue to focus on breathing, Aidan drops his hand and slowly stands up.

He doesn't step away but towers over me.

"You have to give me some answers, Raven."

I can't. I won't.

"Why are you afraid of Gilly?"

My heart threatens to beat out of my chest. I focus on his knees. My hands work along my arms to try to keep me calm. I stop every time I notice but continue when I forget.

"Why did you suggest you wanted to stay in my room?" He fires another question. So many questions that I know he won't allow to go unanswered. Yet, I can't answer any of them. Only one.

"I wanted to share a room with you." I manage to stop touching my arms and look up at Aidan. I bite my cheek to hold back the whimper as his gaze burns my excuse up like dry paper.

"Why?" He grinds his teeth.

"I'm to be your wife." An invisible band tightens around my chest.

He shakes his head. "What exactly will happen when we're in bed at night?" Aidan dips his head as he speaks. "Are you going to fuck me? Can I fuck you?"

His vulgar words have me recoiling from him, yet my core tightens at the thought of having a man like Aidan on top of me. Shame burns my cheeks.

"No," I whisper.

"Then what?" Aidan pushes before he kneels back down. Only this time I don't feel like a queen. I feel like a caged animal that has nowhere to go from here. I can't tell him about the Bratva. He would kill me. Gilly is his cousin. He won't take my word over Gilly's. I have nowhere to go.

Aidan's gaze skips to my lips. Goose bumps break out across my flesh. He said a pretty little thing like me was good for only one thing. *It's only flesh and bone*, I tell myself. *Giving him my body means nothing.*

I lean forward, and he doesn't stop me as I press my lips against his. His warm lips make mine feel cold. My wet hair and damp swimsuit have kept my body temperature low; I hadn't noticed until this moment, and when I place my fingers on Aidan's shoulders, his heat sears my skin. I press nearer to him, shuffling slightly closer to the edge.

Flesh and bone, I remind myself.

It's such a lie. This isn't flesh and bone, especially when Aidan returns the kiss. I feel this right down to my soul. His heat sears the cold, his kiss burns my illusion of distance, and I can't get closer to him. His hands drift down and tug at me. I'm half standing, bent at the waist as I continue to kiss Aidan, continue to lose myself in his touch, kiss, and smell.

I have this brief moment where I know if I don't stop this, I won't be able to. I decide I don't want to. Everything about Aidan is enticing. His hands move to the front of the robe, which he opens with ease. When he touches my waist, with only the swimsuit separating us, I suck in my stomach on reflex. His hands trail down to my bare thighs, and he pushes his tongue into my mouth. I remove my hands from his shoulders and hold his face as I swirl my tongue around his.

My lips slide across his mouth, and I gasp for much-needed air. His hand slips from my outer thigh to my inner one, and I gasp at the contact. Opening my eyes, I look down at Aidan, still on his knees. He's staring up at me with a hunger that has me sandwiching his hand between my legs. He easily pries them open, and he doesn't take his eyes off me as he pushes my red swimsuit aside and sinks one finger inside me. I'm back to gripping his shoulder as my core tightens around his finger. He adds another, while his free hand tightens around my waist, pulling me toward him.

I grip his neck as I throw my head back, and for this moment, I swim in a pool of ecstasy as he adds a third finger. They fill me as his thumb rubs my clit. My stomach swells with a sense of weightlessness. My heart rises to a tempo that has the room dissolving around me. Aidan's fingers move in and out to a rhythm that's slow but pressured. I'm back to looking at him, and I've never wanted to kiss a mouth so much.

His lips are wet, and my core tightens around his fingers again, my wetness growing. Aidan moves faster, and my eyelids flutter closed as I lose myself again. His tempo picks up. My fingers sink into his shoulder as my body warns me that I'm so close to a release I've never felt before. When Aidan presses a kiss to my stomach, I shatter on his fingers. I'm calling out his name with each wave, and when they decrease and stop, I slump forward. He removes his fingers, and I'm wrapped in his arms. I keep my head buried in his chest as I gasp for air. I'm aware of so much. My stomach quivers as I lift my head and look into his eyes.

I have no idea what I see in his eyes, but my body shakes with the intensity of how he watches me. I want him to stop. It's too much. He closes his eyes as I press a kiss to his lips. My hand covers the back of his neck, and his hair dances across my fingers. The length shouldn't be so sexy, but it is. He's sexy. He's like someone who stepped out of a magazine. His sheer beauty is wrong. Yet here he is, kneeling on a floor with me.

When his large hand covers mine, and he moves my fingers close to his large erection, I stop kissing him. Fear that I can't explain slams into me. I'm thinking of Gilly, and I'm scrambling out of Aidan's embrace, leaving him watching me with a dumbfounded expression. I shouldn't do this to him. He has never wronged me. But I also can't stop the fear that pulses through me.

Right now, his brows drag down and his lips part. He's ready to ask me what the fuck is going on, and he has every right to.

I need to say something, anything. "I was married before." That's not what I wanted to say, but I can't take the words back once they leave my lips. Why did I just say that? Panic has me moving back further.

"To the Bratva?" Aidan asks as his Adam's apple bobbles while he waits for me to answer.

Will he kill me?

I nod, unable to say that one simple word. I'm cursing myself for speaking out of turn, but I can't tell him about Gilly. There's no way he would believe me. Gilly being the next to rule also made my complaint irrelevant. There is no one to stand up to him. He has no one to answer to.

He's still staring at me. "When?" His jaw tightens.

Is there any point holding back now? "A year ago. Aidan..."

He holds up his hand, stopping me from speaking, and when he gets to his feet, fear strikes into my heart. I get up too, and I'm unsure of how my legs are supporting me.

"You divorced from the Bratva?" He takes a step closer.

I want to reach down and close my dressing gown, but I'm just barely breathing. I try to stay strong. I try to think of Louise. She needs me. I need to stay strong.

"Yes. I entered a six-month agreement."

Both of Aidan's brows rise, and he stands over me. A storm darkens his gaze, and I want to fly away from him.

I glance to the side, only to have him take my chin in his hand with the fingers that were inside me only moments ago. I can smell myself as he directs my gaze to his.

"Is this a six-month arrangement, too?" His question is so layered, and I'm terrified of what consequence my answer will cause.

CHAPTER TWENTY-ONE

RAVEN

AIDAN GLARES AT ME, and I can't hold his stare. I try to focus on everything around the room, but my gaze seems to revert back to Aidan like some invisible magnetic field pulls at me. When our gazes clash, he releases my chin. My heart pulses rapidly.

"Was he at least good to you?" His question nearly sends my knees buckling. A cry begs to be released, so I twist my lips closed and clamp down on my cheek. A metallic taste floods my mouth.

Aidan takes a step back, his features growing sharper as he clenches his jaw.

The moment he steps away from me, I grip my arms, trying to push the memories that want to surface. They demand for me to relive them over and over again. I push them away, refusing to remunerate.

"He hurt you?" His question sounds more like a statement.

My mouth grows slack. Blood leaves my tongue and brushes against my lips. I quickly lick the blood off, but not before Aidan spots it.

"He did that to your arms?" Aidan's shoulders roll stiffly.

I nod, unable to speak. I'm having an out-of-body experience. I'm watching a car crash but am unable to stop the impact. He continues to watch me, and it's overwhelming to my soul. I blink once, twice. My eyes stay dry, and I swallow, trying to ease my parched throat. My body slumps forward as a wash of dizziness takes over, but I somehow manage to stay upright.

"What's his name?" Aidan asks.

A whimper falls from my lips, and I shake my head. Aidan takes a step toward me with a deadly edge to his eyes. My body finally gives in and crashes. I'm buckling from the inside out as I start to cry. One minute Aidan is glaring at me, the next, I'm in his arms. I cover my face with my hands like I might be able to force back the emotion.

"Shhh," Aidan soothes me. His hands run up and down my back. The gentle contact makes my sobs grow louder.

Aidan holds me until my sobs grow quieter, and when I finally remove my hands from my face, Aidan leans back so he can see me. "You want to tell me why he placed you here?"

I'm shaking my head. Victor placed me here? "My father sent me here." My heart races as Aidan searches my face for a lie. I'm sure he must see the truth, because he releases me.

He's staring at me, waiting for what, I don't know. The thought of Victor placing me here has dread pooling and swirling violently in the pit of my stomach.

"I swear, I don't know what you mean. My father sent me here." I'm repeating my previous statement, as I need him to tell me he got it wrong. That Victor didn't send me here. If he did, this is bad. What could he gain from making me marry Aidan? Did he hope Aidan would abuse me worse than he did? He will be highly disappointed. I'm looking at the man who hasn't laid a finger on me—not without my approval, anyway.

He's never hurt me. Every touch has been gentle. Even now, as he huffs and puffs in front of me with frustration at my lack of information, he doesn't threaten me or try to force the information from me. My stomach squirms with a million butterflies.

Aidan runs his fingers through his hair. "Let's get you set up in my room."

If I had thought for one second that I would be following Aidan out of my own room and into his, I wouldn't have believed it, yet here I am. He keeps glancing at me over his shoulder like he's waiting for me to freak out or change my mind. I am freaking out. My internal reaction to sleeping in the same bed as Aidan is a mixed bag of excitement and fear. But one thing I do know is I won't change my mind. Being away from Gilly is my number one priority. I refuse to put myself in danger. Louise is safe with my auntie, so I can focus on keeping myself as safe as possible.

Aidan opens the double doors that lead into his bedroom. It's not what I'm expecting. I pictured something large, clinical, and contemporary. What I'm walking into is Aidan's life on display. My brain tries to take it all in—the guitar that hangs from the wall, the two more guitars stacked in the corner of the room, paperwork that covers his dressing table, which is what he's gathering up right now. I should try to see if I can catch a glimpse of something, but I'm moving toward the old record player case, which is open.

"The Wolfe Tones," I say, picking up the record and flipping it over. I glance at Aidan from the corner of my eye. He's looking at me now. He gives a quick nod before returning to his dressing table.

I flick through the stack of records that have mostly old Irish rebel music. I can picture Aidan strumming some powerful notes on his guitar, looking as sexy as hell as some woman belts out an old ballad.

I step away from the ancient record player and stop at his chest of drawers. The top has photo albums stacked in a haphazard pile that's ready to tip over. I reach out to open the front cover, when a hand stops me from doing so.

I remove my hand and step away from the dresser as Aidan gathers up the photo albums. I try to keep things light after such heaviness in my room, and I'm also trying to avoid looking at his unmade bed. So, I walk to his guitars in the corner.

"Is it okay if I touch one?" I ask.

Once again, he only nods as he stows all his paperwork and the photo albums into the bedside locker.

I pick up the front one. It's so much heavier than I thought it would be. I run the tips of my fingers across the strings. The noise is instant, and I cover the strings to stop the horrible sound I've created.

"I wouldn't make it in a band," I joke to try to eliminate some of the tension.

There's an awkwardness in Aidan's stance. He glances at the bed. "I'll have Rose make up the bed, and then you can rest."

I take my free hand off the strings and wave it. "No need. I can make the bed."

Aidan is looking from his guitar to the bed.

I have the feeling I need to put it back. He nods in agreement and turns away from me. The minute the door closes, I place the guitar against the wall where it was. Now I'm standing at the edge of his unmade bed. I should check the drawers where he just put his paperwork. Isn't that what he would expect? He could return any second.

Instead, I enter his bathroom, which is mostly white with gold finishings. The room is clinical, like I had thought his bedroom would be. I didn't expect to see pieces of Aidan all around his room. I shower quickly as I think of the artwork hanging on his walls. They didn't belong in a messy room but in a large hall to exhibit how exquisite they are. The artist painted the Irish landscape skillfully.

Once I shower, I wrap myself in a towel and re-enter Aidan's room. I glance at the bed again, and my stomach squeezes. I step up to the first painting and study the backdrop. The sky is perfect: a sheet of blues, and grays that hold a hue of red. In the fields, cows graze. One is done so well that the detail has me smiling, but what makes me laugh is the small cow in the distance, with his tail up in the air like he's ready to poo. The artist has a sense of humor.

The door opens, and my heart slams heavily against my chest. My fingers squeeze the towel, but I relax as Rose steps into the room with a bundle of laundry. "I won't be long. I'm just going to change the bedding."

I can't help but feel a sense of betrayal that Aidan didn't stick to his word and let me make up the bed. The idea of lying under the covers that he lay beneath had excited me.

Lily enters carrying suitcases. "Your clothes, Miss Collins." She doesn't smile, and her formal tone makes me take a step toward her. I want to ask her if she's okay, but Rose reminds her to leave the suitcases in the closet.

"Once you have rested, we will put your garments away," Rose informs me as she swiftly removes the sheets from the bed. Lily does as Rose instructs, and without even glancing at me, she leaves.

Once Rose has made a fresh bed, she draws the curtains across the large three windows before she leaves. The room is darkened, but for the first time since I arrived here, I'm not afraid. It's an odd feeling and has me relaxing so much that I'm ready to sleep.

I quickly search my luggage for underwear and bedclothes. I decide I don't want to be walking around in a small nightdress, so I find a pair of leggings and take one of Aidan's T-shirts off his shelf. His closet is order and perfection, and it's all color coordinated. Once again, the contrast from his bedroom makes me step into his room. I love how it normalizes him. He has likes, dislikes, hobbies, and passions. He isn't just a man who hurts people.

I climb into bed and exhale while looking up at the ceiling. We are all victims of victims. It was something I had seen with Victor. He was so abusive that at the start, I thought if I showed him kindness, he might respond to me differently. That didn't happen. My kindness confused him to the point he lashed out every time. When I tried to protect myself, it made his anger worse, too. I have no idea what happened to him, but he didn't make me a victim. He was a victim too. I know it doesn't justify what he did to me, but that knowledge kept me sane through the worst of times.

I roll onto my side and drag my knees up to my chest. One solitary tear slips out of the corner of my eye. *We are victims of victims.* I recite that knowledge in my head.

With that final thought, I manage to fall asleep.

***

I wake several times, but each time it's brief. I'm alone and the room is darker. Once again, I don't feel fear. I can smell Aidan's cologne, and in my half-asleep state, the scent lulls me back under. When I wake, it's bright in the room. I don't have a phone or a clock, but when I get out of bed and open the curtains, daylight pours in. I slept the whole night. I'm not surprised. Yesterday was exhausting.

My stomach twists. What will Aidan think in the light of day about what he learned yesterday? Will he be angry? Will he have more questions? I glance at the drawer that he stowed the paperwork in, but I'm not brave enough to look, so instead, I get dressed into a blue summer swing dress. The large brown buttons down the front give it a bit of character. I slip into a pair of flat white slippers and make my way into the bathroom. I spend a long time brushing my teeth before washing my face. I'm delaying. Maybe I could hide up here for the day, living in Aidan's world.

As I return to the bedroom, my stomach grumbles. When did I last eat? Yesterday morning, I think. Twenty-four hours. I make my way downstairs. Security is still placed around the house. They don't react to seeing me, but I wonder if Aidan has been informed that I'm on the move. How much freedom do I have, really? Could I snoop around the house without being caught?

I enter the large open kitchen, and Lily is there preparing a tray. Seeing her makes my shoulders relax. She picks up the tray and turns to face me. Her smile is forced, and I'm ready to confront her about her change toward me. I have no idea why she's so cold, but she looks over her shoulder, dips her head, and shoulders past me. I can only imagine who is behind me. It must be Aidan. My heart triples in speed as I turn, but then it stops beating altogether.

"Little Bird." Victor's nickname for me sends my heart into a frenzy, each pulse driving a knife deeper into my soul.

CHAPTER TWENTY-TWO

RAVEN

VICTOR IS HERE, IN Aidan's kitchen. So many emotions slam into me. Fear consumes me at having this monster only a few feet away from me. Did Aidan figure out who Victor was and bring him here to take me back?

A whimper falls from my lips, and I grip my arms. He smiles. "Still the same little bird." He leans in, and I can't do this. I slip past him, and his laughter has me sprinting into the hall. Fear clogs my brain, and I have no idea where I'm running to. All I know is I need to get away from him.

I collide with a solid form that sends me sailing to the ground. The wind is knocked out of me. Jason stands over me, his brows dragging down, and I'm trying to suck in air while scrambling away from him. All I know is I need to hide.

"Raven, what's wrong?" Jason tries to reach for me, but I'm up on my feet, running down a different hallway. The more I pump my legs, the more it drives my fear to a height that threatens to explode.

I see Aidan, and I'm spinning, only to have Jason block me. "What's wrong?" Jason asks again.

I'm shaking my head. They already know. They must know who he is. It's Aidan I focus on. He's within arm's reach. Pain latches onto me and sucks any hope right out of my system.

"Why?" It's the only question I can get out. My body trembles and my vision blurs. "I won't survive," I squeak as the sinking feeling overtakes me. I won't survive. Louise won't survive without me.

The thought of my sister has me pushing against the wall and standing a bit straighter. Aidan has cleared a few more steps and holds out his hands like I'm about to dash. Maybe I am.

"Survive what? What's wrong?" Aidan asks.

"Are you giving me back to him?" I try to hold my head high even as my lip wobbles. Begging isn't beneath me. Aidan has been good to me, and I didn't expect that. "Please. Please don't." I bite the inside of my cheek.

"Victor is only here for a business matter. He isn't here for you." Jason speaks with no emotional attachment.

It's Aidan who seems confused now. "Victor?" he asks Jason.

"Raven's ex-husband."

"You knew." Aidan sounds as betrayed as I felt only moments ago at the idea of Aidan handing me over, and when Aidan extracts a gun from the inside of his suit jacket, I push down the truths that Gilly shared with me. He said that Aidan would kill Victor, then me.

The gun looks huge in Aidan's hand. His fingers rest on the trigger, and a coldness settles on my flesh, sending the hairs rising along my body. Pins prick every single piece of me, and I'm slammed with the knowledge that this is my end.

Is there anything I can say that will make a difference?

"Don't do this." Jason widens his eyes and holds up his hands like he thinks Aidan will shoot him. Jason is still blocking the hallway.

"Move out of my way." Aidan's voice is barely a whisper, and when he raises the gun, I scream. I can't accept this.

Aidan flashes me a look.

Jason points at me. "You're terrifying her."

"Like you give a fuck!" Aidan's anger fills the hallway, and I'm glued to the wall like I can escape his fury. I can't. Aidan points at me. "You don't give two shits if she lives or dies."

Jason takes a step toward Aidan and drops his hands. "You're right, I don't. But you do. If you kill Victor, you will start a war. A war she won't survive." Jason is back to pointing at me.

Two things happen to me at once. First, I realize that Aidan isn't going to shoot me or hand me back to

Victor. The second is that Aidan wants to shoot Victor for hurting me.

"Get him the fuck out of my home. If I go back outside, I will kill him."

Jason is nodding. "I'll take care of it." Jason takes one final look at me before he leaves me alone with Aidan.

I swallow my fear and step away from the wall. My gaze darts from Aidan's stoic expression to the hand that still holds the gun.

"Aidan." I say his name so gently, and he looks at me. He works a muscle in his jaw and puts away the gun. He won't look at me as he speaks. "Let's get you upstairs."

I don't object. I don't want to be anywhere near Victor. We don't take the main stairs. Instead, Aidan opens a door, which I assume leads to a closet, but I'm surprised to see a stairwell. I look up at the circular wrought-iron stairs.

"It's for the staff," he informs me as he stays at the base of the stairs to let me go first. The circular steps take us to another door, and I open it. We arrive out onto the landing. The minute Aidan closes the door behind us, I take a peek. A picture hangs on either side of the door, and I wonder if that is intentional.

Aidan is waiting for me. Once again, he isn't looking at me, but once I step close to him, he walks to his room and opens the doors to let me enter. Aidan doesn't come in but grips the handles like he's ready to leave me.

"Please don't leave." My words come out in a rush. He still won't look at me, but he hasn't left, either.

"Please, Aidan."

His gaze finally lands on me. I have no idea what he's thinking, but I win. He enters the room and closes the door behind him.

An awkward tension has me feeling uncertain now. My emotions are a tangled mess. I'm reliving that moment with Victor in the kitchen.

"I thought he was here for me," I say and fold my arms across my chest.

"This isn't helping, Raven." Aidan's snarl surprises me. He still won't look at me. "If you keep talking about him, I'm going to leave this room and kill him."

I'm nodding vigorously. "So, you play the guitar?" I ask.

He narrows his eyes before looking away. He's ready to bolt and make good on his promise. I'd let him, but Jason said it would cause a war.

"Will you play something for me?" I ask.

Aidan exhales loudly. "No." He looks at me again, and this time when his gaze lingers on me, I feel so bare. He's seeing the worst of me, the damaged, scarred girl, and I don't want him to just see that. I want him to see more of me.

"I had a brother." I admit something that I've never told anyone. "Eric. He was all smiles. Like..." I frown for a moment as I picture his smiling face. "Like a ridiculous amount of smiles. My father used to smile at him."

Aidan relaxes slightly.

I give a short laugh with relief. "I know that's hard to believe." I unfold my arms. "He was six months old when he died." Eric, the ray of sunshine that actually brought light to our home. When he died...

"I'm sorry, Raven." Aidan's voice deepens and cracks.

"We were lucky to have the time we had with him." I exhale some of the emotion. "It was a long time ago."

I take a shaky step toward Aidan. "He was so tiny, and yet, he made us smile. Even my father, who didn't know how to express joy. At the time, I just saw him as a smiling baby, but now I see him as a sign of hope."

Aidan frowns. "How so?"

"That kindness is more powerful than cruelty. That a smile can cause a smile."

Aidan takes a step toward me. "All I hear is the death of a baby."

He diverts his gaze again, and I fear I've lost him. When he looks at the door like he wants to leave, I step up to him and do something not just for him, but for me too. I wrap my arms around his waist. He's stiff and doesn't respond at first, but he also doesn't try to detangle from me. He's angry, too angry to be allowed to leave this room. I would love for Victor to die, but after Jason's warning about causing a turf war, I realize I don't want to lose Aidan. The thought has my stomach plummeting, and I tighten my hold on him.

His arms slowly rise and wrap around me. When his chin rests on the crown of my head, I inhale him. His unique smell. The heat from his body warms me, scaring away all the cold. My cheeks heat as my mind goes to how it feels to have Aidan kissing me, and when I take my head off his chest and look up at him, he's staring down at me. A hunger darkens his eyes.

"I want you to make me a promise." His voice is gravelly.

I'm nodding in agreement. Right now, I'd promise him anything to keep him looking at me.

"One day, not now, you will tell me what Victor did to you."

I flinch, and Aidan's arms tighten around my waist. "Promise me."

He has no idea what he's asking, or maybe he does. I nod again. "I promise."

A sad smile twists his lips, and he raises a hand and cups my cheek. I lean into his touch, and my lids flutter closed. His lips fit mine perfectly, and he's the cure. The cure to the sickness that's Victor. My body grows light again, and I can't help the vision of blue waters flowing over hot coals, dousing the flames, caressing the pain, and taking all the heat away. I grip Aidan's shoulders to pull his mouth heavier against mine, and he bends to my will.

My fingers slide to the collar of his shirt. His flesh is warm, his neck soft, but the sharpness of his few-days'-old beard brushes against my palm. The sensation drives both my hands to his face. He breaks the kiss and leans forward against me. I don't want this to stop. I stand on the tip of my toes to press a kiss to his lips, but he doesn't let me reach his mouth.

"I won't hold back this time," he tells me.

A thrill races through me.

"I want you," he confesses, and my knees buckle a little; my heart soars, and I'm nodding.

His mouth brushes against mine. "Tell me you want me too."

Do I? I'm looking into his eyes, and this close, I can see small flecks of gold dance and swirl. I really think about what he's saying. Every single part of me wants Aidan. I nod, knowing that this moment will change everything.

"I want you too," I admit.

CHAPTER TWENTY-THREE

AIDAN

"SAY THAT AGAIN," I prompt. I never thought words would turn me on so much.

"I want you." Raven doesn't shy away but looks up into my eyes. I love how my hand encases her cheek.

She takes in a sharp breath as I drag her mouth to mine. I inhale her scent, my cock hardening. I could make this a game, a challenge to see how long I can hold out. Letting my hand run to the back of her neck, I probe at the top of her spine. Raven's eyes widen before they flutter closed. She leans in until our lips brush against each other.

Small hands ball up my shirt as Raven uses her strength to drag me closer. I want the same thing. I release her neck and easily lift her off the ground. My hand finds its way under her dress as I carry her wedding style to the bed. Her lips leave mine, her gaze soaking me up, and I smile down at her.

I reach the bed, but instead of placing her down, I climb up, keeping her in my arms. Her small hands still fist my shirt. Blue eyes that have never looked so innocent stare up at me with anticipation.

One thing I know is I won't disappoint. I release her and lower her into the center of the bed. The large brown buttons on the front of her dress pop open with ease. They stop at her navel, and I push the fabric aside to take in her breasts and flat stomach. I spread my fingers across her stomach, and she inhales a sharp lungful of air. The idea of a life growing inside her has my cock straining against my trousers. I never thought much of having children, but with Raven lying under me with a look of awe in her eyes, I want something deeper to connect us, like a life given, not taken.

I remove my hand from her stomach. Gripping the edge of her dress, I drag the material up to her waist. She raises her hands to allow me to pull the dress off.

"Perfection," I say.

She quickly tries to fold her arms like she might be able to cover up the scars. I grip her wrists and pin them to the bed, straddling her.

"Don't ever hide from me," I whisper, and before she can answer, I bend my neck and kiss the scars that run the length of her arms. I can't focus on them without the anger taking over. Releasing her wrists, I continue to kiss down her side and plant promises on her stomach that I will fill her with my seed.

Her hands rest on my shoulders, and I feel the pressure as she lifts her core upward. I grin as I kiss further down and press one kiss to the band of her panties. She inhales another sharp breath.

I make my way back up and kneel so Raven can watch me as I strip off my shirt. She drinks in every inch of my chest, but she doesn't move or attempt to touch me. When I remove my trousers and my erection springs free, her eyes widen, and this time she half sits up. My cock throbs, the head swollen and red with a need to be inside her. When she reaches out and touches me, I bend forward.

"Fuck," I groan. Her fingers run the length of my shaft, and she shimmies closer so she can tighten her hand around my cock. I don't want to come this way, but if she keeps stroking me, I will. "Lie back," I command. She doesn't comply straight away but continues to stroke my cock.

"Now, Raven," I growl. The power in her eyes makes me lean in and kiss her. "I need to be inside you."

I press another kiss to her mouth before she lies back down. She spreads her legs, bending them with a need to have me inside her. I don't remove her small white panties. The urgency to fill her has me pulling them aside. Placing my shaft at her opening, she pushes her hips high and presses upon my cock.

Her tightness around my cock has me groaning, and when she groans too, I feel the shift of power as I push in and out of Raven. Gripping her thighs, I keep her legs high to give myself full access. Fucking her this way lets me see her.

Raven keeps looking at me as I sink into her. Her want propels me to move faster into her. I'm so close to coming, but I don't want this to end.

She throws her head to the side, her breaths quickening, her body jerking as she nears her release. I move faster and press my hand to her stomach. Her head snaps back to me, and she cries out as she comes. Her ecstasy feeds into mine, and I pump one, two, three, times as I come inside her. A few more thrusts, and the satisfaction I feel has me leaning down and stroking Raven's damp hair. She appears feverish, and I love that I put that look on her face. I press a kiss to the tip of her nose as our breaths mingle and swirl together.

"I promise I will find a way to kill Victor." I make my promise while still buried inside her.

Raven's stares at me; she's ready to shake her head.

"You don't have to say anything, Raven." I press another kiss to her lips like I can seal the promise.

It takes me some time before I finally extract myself from her. She hasn't said much, and I don't force her as she pulls the sheets across her body. I go to the bathroom and return with a washcloth. As I walk around the side of the bed, Raven's gaze tracks me. When I reach for the covers, she doesn't stop me as I pull them back.

My cock twitches as I spread her legs. She lifts her hips for me as I remove her panties before cleaning her.

"Why don't you rest?" I say once I'm finished.

She nods but chews on her lip. "He used a belt to beat me."

Everything in me turns to ice before it melts faster than calcium chloride melts ice. I'm burning up with pure, undiluted rage. The fucking animal.

Raven's hand rises, and she touches her neck. "He used the belt to choke me."

She won't look at me when she says the next line. "He raped me."

I sink down on the bed and take her hand like it's annealed glass. "He won't. Ever. Hurt. You. Again." Each word sounds sharp and volatile. So I take a calming breath. "He will die for what he has done," I promise gently.

Raven blinks a stray tear before she nods. "Thank you."

I'm shaking my head. Why would she thank me? What he did to her brings me back full circle as to why she was placed here. What is he planning? My gut tightens with uncertainty. The only way to know is to ask the source. Once Victor tells me, I can kill him. I just need to make sure his death isn't traced back to me. Otherwise, I would have shot him in the face earlier.

I can't start a war. I lean down and press a kiss to Raven's forehead. "I'll take care of you now," I tell her.

Her eyelids flutter closed, and the look of contentment on her face has me pressing another kiss to the side of her head.

My phone rings, breaking the moment. Raven's eyes spring open. I get up and walk around to my trousers strewn on the floor. Removing my phone, I'm surprised to see William's number flash up on the screen. I answer the call.

"Everything okay?" I ask straight away, because with William, things normally aren't okay.

"Yeah, I was just wondering if you had time to talk."

William's voice sounds different. I'm not sure why, but there's something different in his tone that has me glancing at Raven. She's wrapped the blankets around herself and is watching me.

"We could meet at Fifty/Fifty," William says. The restaurant our father loved.

I know this must be important, as William never seeks me out to talk, but going off right now and leaving Raven doesn't sit right with me.

"Could you come to my house?" I think of a compromise.

"I can be there in an hour."

My shoulders relax. "See you then." I hang up and turn to Raven. "My brother William is coming soon."

I walk toward her, and her gaze takes in my nakedness.

"Move over," I say.

Her cheeks heat, but she slides over, and I lie beside her. My cock demands I take her again, but there's too much vulnerability about Raven right now. I pat my chest. "Lie with me."

She smiles and rests her head on my chest. I wrap my arm around her and just hold her. Her knee brushes my cock, and I grit my teeth, forcing myself not to react. I stay with Raven until my phone rings again.

It's Donald informing me of William's arrival. Once I'm dressed, I press a kiss to Raven's lips. She's fast asleep, and I pull the blankets up around her shoulders before I leave. I'm sure seeing Victor took everything out of her. If I had known who he was, I wouldn't have let him near her.

I clear the final step to find Donald waiting for me.

"Master Murphy. William is in the conservatory."

That's strange, and a bad feeling settles over me. William has never gone into that room, because it was Father's favorite.

"Thank you, Donald." I walk quickly, wanting to know what's wrong. Now that my head is clearer, I start to worry about Matty. Is that why William is here? To bring me bad news about one of our siblings?

The minute I reach the conservatory, I want him to tell me straight away what's happened. Maybe he senses the urgency as he spins around and speaks.

"Everyone is fine."

I nod and take him in. He appears different. His gaze is clear, yet troubled. But he's in a suit, and he's never looked so much like one of us as he does right now.

"Good. I found it odd you picked this room," I say as I sit down in Father's chair.

William stiffens, reaching up and pulling a leaf off a plant above his head. "It seemed appropriate."

I settle into the seat, and I'm tempted to check the time. I want to get back to Raven. The thought startles me. My time has always been reserved for my family and no one else. So the thought is foreign to me.

"I haven't been drinking," William confesses.

That's why he looks different. He doesn't have the usual slurred smirk or the dangerous edge to him. He seems troubled, like he knows what's happening around him for the first time. It's clear it's not a nice place to be for William. But since Father died, that's all he has done—drink.

"I'm proud of you, Will."

His brows drag down into an angry frown. He dismisses my praise with a raise of his hand. "There is nothing to be proud of. I drank because I couldn't accept what I saw." William speaking of finding our father has me sitting straighter.

"No one could, William. Finding that..." *Would destroy anyone*. Of course, I don't finish that sentence.

"It wasn't finding Father." William rolls the leaf he plucked in between his thumb and forefinger. "I mean, yeah, I can't get the image out of my head. You know." His foot jangles, and I see all the layers of damage.

"I'm fucking sorry, William." I stand up, wanting to erase some of the torture I see in his gaze.

"It had to be one of us, right?" He gives a pained smile.

"I wish it hadn't been you," I admit.

"Why?" He crushes the leaf between his fingers. "You think you would handle it any better?"

I'm ready to tell him that's not what I meant, but he continues.

"You think when you noticed how he had no scratch marks on his neck that it wouldn't fuck with your head? Hmm. He didn't even try to stop it from happening. He kept his hands at his sides."

"What you saw—"

"You have no idea of what I fucking saw." His voice rises, and I stuff my hands into my pockets. I'm ready to push back to make him calm down, but William gathers himself. It's something I'm not used to seeing him do. "None of that matters. What matters is the rope. It had three double knots in it."

I shrug. "So what?" What did it matter how he tied the rope?

William grins, and I see life in his eyes that I haven't seen before. "You remember going boating with him?"

I nod and remove my hands from my pockets. "Yeah. The last time we went, Alex had a cold and he couldn't come."

William laughs. "Yeah, you and Jason gave him such a hard time for that."

I'm smiling too. We really had, but it didn't make him come. My memories of the boat trip float through my mind as William continues to speak.

"You remember asking Dad to tie a knot and he failed miserably?"

My stomach plummets and hairs rise along my arms. "That was two weeks before he died," I whisper.

William's smile is manic. "Exactly. This rope had three double knots. He didn't hang himself."

I don't ask William what he's suggesting, because it's as clear as day. He thinks our father was murdered, and his death was staged to look like a suicide.

I run my hand along the back of my neck to try to shake off the uncertainty of who we can trust. Who did this to us? To our father?

"He was murdered, Aidan." William is so close to me, and I see it, the relief in his eyes. Could he just be seeing things that he wants to see? I need to see the rope.

Before I can ask more, my phone rings. I take it out and am surprised to see Detective Regs's name flash up on my screen.

He's on our payroll, and I wonder if he came to the same conclusion that William has somehow.

I answer the call. "Regs, it's been a while."

"This isn't a social call."

I turn away from William. "It never is."

Sirens blare in the background. "Celine Collins was found dead in her home an hour ago."

Fuck.

CHAPTER TWENTY-FOUR

RAVEN

MY MOTHER'S DEATH SHAKES me in a way I didn't think it would. I blame myself. I should have protected her better. After I had provoked my father to hit me, I knew the action wouldn't go unpunished. All I had thought about was Louise, and knowing she was safe with my aunt had given me strength. Clearly, my mother took the brunt of his anger, and from the scratch marks on his neck, she fought back.

Tears fall as I walk behind the hearse. Louise's arm links mine. The last few days have been a blur. When Aidan woke me with the news, I just accepted everything he told me. It took days before reality hit me and my pain finally came to the surface.

Louise squeezes my arm like she's the grown-up here and needs to comfort me. She does look so different in a fitted black dress. I hadn't noticed how developed she's become. She's a young woman. Maybe I just hadn't wanted to notice that she's no longer the child I claim her to be. Next week she turns sixteen, but she appears a lot older.

The streets have been cleared for the funeral, but on either side of our procession, people stand silently at the road side in a show of respect. Aidan walks beside me. He looks so handsome in a suit, and I don't think I could have made it through the past week without him.

"She's at peace," Louise says. Her voice quivers and guilt churns in my stomach. Her ending was violent, and my father would never pay for what he did. I glance at him over my shoulder. He plays the part of a mourning widower. He makes me sick.

I tighten my hold on Louise. "She would be so happy to see us together," I say.

Louise rests her head on my shoulder. The hearse slows as it pulls into the graveyard. Aidan's large hand takes mine as we proceed at a snail's pace down the pathway. We stop at the freshly dug grave. He leans in and presses a kiss on my cheek. "I'll be right behind you," he says.

I don't want him to go, but it's a tradition that only the family stands at the grave. I nod and blink some falling tears away.

My father takes Aidan's place, and I would love nothing more than to push him into the fucking hole.

Louise is stiff beside me as they remove the coffin from the hearse and lower the wooden box into the ground. Prayers are spoken above the soil, and our tears are met by the wind that's whipped up.

The first shovel of clay makes me jump, and I close my eyes, asking my mother for forgiveness. I should have thought of her. I shouldn't have provoked my father. I glance at him, but he's already turning away from the grave and joining some of his work colleagues I've seen around the house. Their low chat and rumbled laughter have me taking a step toward them.

I release Louise and take another step. He can't do this. A shadow falls over me as Aidan steps in my way. Without a word, he takes my face in his hand and smiles down at me. It's a knowing smile that accompanies a kiss on my lips.

"Introduce me to your sister."

I know what he's doing. He's trying to stop me from confronting my father.

I allow it and turn to Louise, who watches us with a genuine smile, even as tears are wet on her cheeks. Louise had arrived with Father, so I didn't have time to introduce them.

"Louise, this is Aidan."

My sister takes Aidan's outstretched hand. "Hi." Louise's voice is soft and a little shaky.

"Lovely to finally meet you." He takes her hand. "Raven never stops talking about you."

I fight a smile. It's true; the last few days all I could think about was Louise, and I ended up reminiscing about all the good times we had. Aidan had sat and listened into the late hours of the night to my whole childhood with Louise.

"All good, I hope?" Louise says, looking from me to Aidan.

"I really enjoyed the story about the coal bunker."

Louise's eyes widen with horror and she glares at me. "You didn't?" Her outrage has Aidan chuckling.

I nod to clarify. I did tell the story of how she had gotten into the coal bunker naked, not a stitch of clothes on her. She was black as coal, literally. Our mother freaked. It took weeks to get the black coal out from under her nails.

We are all sober as people start to give their condolences, and I remember why we are here. After we shake hands with most people, we move to the reception my father is hosting in one of his hotels. The room is full, and he moves around it like he's the host of a celebration and not the death of his wife. She's buried now, so he doesn't care.

He should be rotting behind bars, but I'm not foolish. I've seen enough to know that men like him can bury all their dirty secrets, and there's always someone on standby with a shovel.

Aidan sits with me and Louise, and I'm surprised when he tells Louise he used to be in a band and played the lead guitar.

"You don't look like someone in a band," Louise admits.

"If I hadn't seen his guitars with my own eyes, I wouldn't believe him either." I can't help but smile at Aidan. My stomach squirms. He's been my rock, and the turnaround since I met him has been everything. He smiles back at me.

"Maybe later I'll play you both a song."

I'd squeal with excitement, but instead I nod.

Aidan rises and presses a kiss on my forehead. "I'll give you ladies some time. Gary will keep people away." Just as he says the words, he signals for Gary, his bodyguard, to come over.

"Make a perimeter around them. Let them have time to speak."

I'm ready to tell Aidan that isn't necessary, but something in Louise's eyes makes me stop. I don't want to ask what is wrong because we are at our mother's funeral, but I get the sense that it's more.

"He loves you," Louise says while she stirs a cup of tea.

I love him too. It's an odd feeling to have. I don't say the words. "He's been good to me," I admit.

Louise glances up at me. "He's more than good," Louise declares as she looks at the wide circle of security that protects us from people who veer toward us only to be redirected away.

"I hate Father," she comments while looking out at the crowd. "I hate him so much."

Shivers assault my body. I reach for her hand and she pulls away, stopping me, confusing me.

"I'm serious." Her jaw is clenched, and I've never seen Louise like this before.

"Did he threaten you?" I grip my sister's arm, making her look at me.

Her gaze fills with tears. "He already tried to hurt me, just..." Her face twists with pain. "When he found out Mam had sent me to Auntie Amanda's, he sent for me. Once I arrived back, he was in the worst form I've ever seen."

She's looking out into the crowd. The buzzing around us disappears again as she looks at me. "He was hurting me, and she stepped in."

I inhale a sharp breath. No. No. No. Please God, don't tell me she witnessed our mother's death.

"She fought back." Louise cries, and I pull her into a hug.

I hug her only for a moment, as she pushes me away and turns to pick up her tea. All her tears are hidden, but she can't stop the anger I see flash across her features. My sister is all grown up and has been treated in the worst way.

"You shouldn't have seen that," I tell her.

She won't look at me. "Well, I did," she responds just as someone breaks the circle.

It's our father.

"My daughters." He sits down with a smile on his face.

He glances at the perimeter around us before leaning into me. "I would suggest you tell your fiancé to call off his watchdogs. You're making my guests feel uneasy."

I twist my hands together in my lap. The marks on his neck make my stomach churn. I take a peek at Louise. She's paler than before, and her hands tremble along with her lip. I should be protecting her. How? I have nothing to offer my sister. I can't take her away. I have nothing. I need to get my father the information he wants. That means betraying Aidan. Pain that rattles me has me digging my nails into my palm.

"You said when I got you the information, that me and Louise would be free?"

My father's features tighten. He's ready to speak.

"Just answer me," I snarl, wanting to hurt him so badly.

He's glaring at me. He wants to react to my anger with his own, but he's aware we aren't alone.

He forces a smile. "Of course."

"I'll get something soon," I promise.

Louise shakes her head. "Raven—"

"Trust me," I tell her.

She's watching me with so much uncertainty in her gaze. But she finally nods. "I trust you."

My father snorts, gaining my attention again.

"I hope you have a really good story for the scratch marks on your neck." I shouldn't provoke him, but I can't not say anything.

"A wild cat." He stands up like he's won. "Not far from the truth."

"Louise will stay with me for the next few days." I raise my chin.

He laughs before bending down. "That's not going to happen. Bring me information, and you can take her." He starts to walk away but pauses. "And get rid of this ridiculous circle of security." He leaves this time. I can't glance at my sister. I don't want to see the look on her face.

"Raven, please don't do anything stupid." Louise's voice is low.

I try to rein in my fear and smile at her. "I promise."

A smile dances on her lips. "You will do it no matter what I say."

I take my sister's hand. "We will be free soon."

She turns her head away from me.

"Please, Louise, look at me."

She does, slowly.

"I promise I'll get you as soon as I can."

She nods, and her chin wobbles with emotion. She pulls her hand from mine, and I hate that I can't do anything right now.

I stand and tell Gary we're done. The circle of security melts away, and like a barrier falling, people veer toward us. We chat with everyone, and time stretches out for far too long.

My father is the first to depart, and he calls Louise to leave with him. Before she leaves, I pull her into a hug.

"Please don't forget me," she whispers as she steps away.

She's all I've ever thought of.

I don't look away until the door closes, and I can no longer see her.

A hand snakes around my waist. I don't have to look to know it's Aidan. His touch has me leaning into his side.

"You look ready to collapse. Let me take you home." He presses a kiss on the crown of my head.

Home. I nod, unable to do anything else. When I get this information for my father, I'll have to leave Aidan. I grit my teeth together. Aidan leaves me with Gary as he retrieves my bag and jacket. He's only gone a moment, and when he returns and places his hand on the small of my back, I would give anything not to have to betray him.

I wipe at a falling tear quickly, but not quickly enough. Aidan applies more pressure on my back as he guides me outside and into the waiting limo. The minute we're in, he pulls me into his side, and the driver closes the door. The world is gone, and it's just us. I start to cry, and Aidan holds me. I don't stop, even as the car starts to move. I don't just cry for my mother. I cry for what I must do and the idea of giving up Aidan. I swallow the panic and fear and take my head off his chest.

"I can tell you it doesn't get easier with time." His honesty makes me choke on a pained laugh. Most people say time heals all. "But with time, you learn to deal with it better."

It makes me think of his father. I reach up and touch his handsome face. "Were you close to your father?"

His jaw clenches under my fingers. I think he won't answer me, but he does. "Yes. We all were. He was a great father. He taught us everything about the business. He took us fishing."

Pain twists Aidan's features. "He laughed so much," Aidan dwindles off.

"I'm so sorry." I run my thumb along his cheek.

"I'm sorry too," he says before pressing his lips to mine. The kiss ignites a fire low in my belly, and I grip his face like I need to memorize everything about him, and I do. This may be the last time I'm with him.

I tug up my dress and straddle him. Aidan's hands immediately go to my hips. The heat of his skin burns through the dress. I hold his face and look down at him. My hair falls around us like a veil. My heart triples in speed as emotions demand to be released. We are frozen in each other's gaze, drawing the essence of what makes us up, and with just a look, I want to crumble and tell him everything, but no matter what, I can't tell a Mafia man that the only reason I'm marrying him is to steal from him. I know if I get caught, the sentence is death.

A shiver snakes along my spine, and I slam my mouth onto Aidan's, not wanting to think about betrayal or stealing or death sentences.

His fingers slide under the hem of my dress easily and work their way to my core. I lift my body and reach down until I graze his erection. He inhales at the contact.

I pause, remembering we are in a limo. I'm looking at the blackout window that divides us from the driver.

"Don't worry. They won't disturb us. They can't see or hear us," he adds.

That's good enough for me. When I face him, he grins, and it's a grin that promises to devour me. I want him to. He grips my neck and drags my lips back to his mouth, and I let go of anything that was holding me back, giving in to the want that's driving me to reach down and open the buckle of his belt. Aidan helps me and pushes his trousers down slightly. Pushing up my dress until it's wrapped around my stomach, he pulls my panties aside before placing his cock at my opening. I grind down the moment his hand is out of my way. Gripping the headrest behind us, I hold tight and pull my body up and down on top of Aidan. He grips my waist to help guide me. I continue to kiss him, and when his tongue slips into my mouth, the kiss grows as frantic as my thrusts on top of him. It started out with me doing the work, but now, Aidan lifts me and slams me down, controlling the fast pace that threatens to take both of us to the edge.

I'm aware of the limo slowing, and it causes me to slow too.

"Don't stop," Aidan growls, and his need has me closing my eyes and matching his rhythm again. I'm so close, and when he pushes up inside me and pauses as his seed flows freely, I move down and let go. My orgasm is all-consuming, and I'm shaking as I continue to come on Aidan.

Aidan kisses me softly, and I can't bear to meet his eyes. So I climb off him and fix my dress. He pulls up his trousers. His phone buzzes, and Aidan reads the message. His body stiffens and I reach out, touching his leg.

"Is everything okay?" I ask.

He shoves the phone into his pocket. "Yes, everything is fine." And when he leans forward and taps on the glass a few seconds later, my door opens. "You go ahead. I have to head out for a few hours."

I don't get out straight away. I have this terrible sense of foreboding, like all this between us is about to change.

"Raven?" Aidan's question has me forcing a smile as I glance at him over my shoulder.

"I'm going to get some sleep. I'll see you later."

"I'll be as quick as I can." He moves across the seat and brushes a kiss on my cheek.

I get out before I lose any strength I have gained. All I have to do is conjure an image of Louise, and I'm moving into the house. I stay at the door as I watch the red lights grow further away. I will never get a chance like this again.

I'm in luck tonight. I don't see any staff in the halls or security. Everything is on my side. And when I step up to Aidan's office door, the handle turns easily in my hand. I take one final look up and down the hallway before I enter.

Closing the door softly behind me, I turn on the lights. Every instinct I have tells me to leave. Tells me not to do this. But I need to protect Louise.

I'm at the desk pulling open drawers, but I find nothing. The filing cabinet is also unlocked, and it's starting to feel a lot less like luck, and I'm becoming increasingly suspicious. My heart starts to race as a picture protrudes from the wall. I stand and realize it's coming forward only on the right side, like a door.

I'm walking quickly over to the picture and swing it on the hinges that anchor it to the wall. A safe is behind it. My chest tightens. Would he have all his plans inside? The safe is code protected. I have no idea what that code could be. I stare so long at the keypad that I don't hear anyone enter.

"What are you doing?" Jason's voice renders me frozen.

Oh, God, no. I've been caught.

CHAPTER TWENTY-FIVE

Aidan

LEAVING RAVEN ON THE night of her mother's funeral doesn't sit well with me. I would have never left her, only Gary informed me that Victor was staying in one of Raven's father's hotels. Right now, he has only two security guards stationed outside his door.

This is an opportunity I can't let slip past. The limo slows as we pull up at the hotel. Walking through the front doors isn't wise. I lean forward and knock on the dividing window. My reflection disappears as the divider rolls down. "Park in the underground parking," I instruct.

My driver nods, and we pull around the back of the hotel. The underground parking won't have many people around. That's my hope. I remove my gun, knowing I won't get past his security with the weapon on me. I also remove my phone and leave it sitting on the seat. I'm tempted to ring Jason and see how Raven is. He and Frank are in the house. For two entirely different reasons. Jason is there to make sure Raven is okay.

Frank is doing what Frank does best. Killing people. He favors my home for his messy jobs, maybe because it was always the hub when father was alive.

"If I'm not back in twenty minutes, leave. Inform Jason where I am." My gut tightens. Jason won't approve. But if they kill me, at least they know where to collect my body. I get out of the car and spot two cameras. I keep my head down and walk behind the barriers until I reach the stairwell. Floor four, room one hundred and twenty-one. That's where Victor is staying.

There are no cameras or people in the stairwell. I take two steps at a time until I reach the door to the fourth floor. I slow down and take off my suit jacket. I leave it in the corner of the small landing before pulling open the door. The fourth floor is quiet. The wide hallways tell me this is where the rich stay. I pass a waiter pushing a trolley. His dark hair is slicked back, and he greets me with a bob of his head.

"Have a good night, sir." He doesn't slow down.

"Thank you," I respond and keep walking. It's easy to spot Victor's room without even reading the number on the door. Two large men with stoic faces and folded arms block the double doors.

I slow my footing as I near them.

"I'm here to see Victor."

I'm waiting for them to ask me who I am or to tell me to go away because Victor is busy, but instead, the one closest to the door steps forward.

"Raise your arms."

I do, and he pats me down. Once he's sure I have no weapons, the other security man opens the door for me to enter. That's not good. Without as much as blinking, the security waits for me to make up my mind.

I've one shot at this. I step forward and walk into Victor's suite. I'm tense, waiting to be jumped. When the door closes, I glance over my shoulder. But there's no one behind me.

"It's just us." Victor's Russian accent slithers under my skin. I face forward, where his voice drifts from. He's sitting on the couch, arms spread out on either side of him. He's a big man. Six foot five inches at least. Raven must have been terrified. Victor isn't someone I'd normally go against. Most certainly not without a gun or two.

"Were you expecting me?" I ask, hating having to engage in conversation with him.

His blond hair is almost white, and he grins, dropping his arms. "Yes, I was. When you didn't return to our meeting at your home, I knew you would eventually come." He points at a seat across from him.

"I've come to kill you," I say.

He laughs and sits forward. I won't be able to wrap my hands around his thick neck, but I'd love to.

"Not when I tell you all about Raven."

I don't give two shits about what he has to say about Raven. Beating her... I grit my teeth. Raping her.

"You raped her." My voice is low, deadly. My heart drums.

Victor sits back, his smile is gone. "I had a right to her. She was my wife."

He doesn't deny raping her, and that gives me even more comfort at killing him.

"She's a thief. She stole plans from my home, and her father used them to secure property that was rightfully mine," Victor grits out, his Russian accent becoming thicker with his annoyance. "He made a fool of me. She made a fool of me."

I raise a brow, asking him silently if I look like I give a fuck.

"You know we're helping Frank take down the O' Reagans." Victor shifts gears.

"Good luck with that." For the first time, I hope Shay and Richard O'Reagan wipe out the Bratva.

"We have already taken one down."

This surprises me. I hadn't heard of an O'Reagan falling—something I'll ask about after I kill Victor. "Congratulations. Which one? I highly doubt Shay or Richard has fallen." If they had, we would have heard about it.

Victor laughs. "So very hostile. Warren O'Reagan. He's a small fish, but he's still an O'Reagan. I'll stop busting your balls and tell you the truth about Raven, since that is really why you are here. I had Frank place Raven in your home so we could catch her red-handed stealing again. When she does, I get to punish her."

My whole body tenses. She would never steal from me. "You would have no right to punish my wife," I announce.

His slimy smile makes my nerves jangle.

"That's what you don't see in the fine print. She is still my wife. I just need to catch her in the act. I want her to pay for what she did to me."

He's lying. The uncomfortable words make me shift in my seat.

"Don't tell me you have fallen for her lies." He gets up and walks to a bar in the corner of the room. Would she really steal from me?

He pours out two small glasses of vodka. "Gilly is keeping a close eye on her for me. So when she steps out of line, he will report back."

I stand up. Everything about this conversation disturbs me.

"Why have Gilly lead the Mafia?" I have to ask. It makes no fucking sense.

Victor doesn't smile with delight at the question like I thought he would. His face is stoic, and he knocks back his vodka. When he's done, he pushes the small glass toward me. I get up and meet him at the bar.

"That wasn't my call. That came from higher up."

I knock the vodka back. "You just do as you're told." I grin.

He doesn't like that one bit, but he refills his drink. As he downs the vodka, I smash my glass into the side of his face. He stumbles back, not expecting the hit.

I've used the element of surprise, but now it's gone, and this big fucking Russian is pissed and reaching for something under the bar, which is no doubt a gun. I jump up on the bar and slam my feet into Victor's chest. He's a fucking beast of a man, and when he falls, he takes down half the bar with him. The roar of crashing bottles and glasses has the double doors opening. I have to act quickly. Victor is still under broken glass, so I focus on the immediate threat.

I get a glimpse at his security, who have their guns ready as they scan the room. I dive forward and pull the gun that Victor was reaching for out of the holster. The silenced weapon fires off a shot, and the first security hits the ground. The second returns fire, until Victor shouts in Russian. He doesn't stay down long. The minute he speaks, I pivot, but not before he drags me back through the glass, his arms like a vise around my throat. My side burns, but I ignore the pain. I turn the gun and pull the trigger, but miss his face. I can't see his security, and as I struggle against Victor's arm, I try to track any movement in the room. My vision dips, and Victor roars as his arms tighten on my throat. The sound brings his security into view, and I use my focus to shoot him clean in the chest before I slam my head back into Victor's face.

He cries out and his hold loosens on me. I turn the gun on him, and he grabs at it too, giving me enough wiggle room to get out of his arms. His strength has him winning the gun, but before he pulls the trigger, I get a hit to his face. I can't get the gun, so I hit it out of his hand and watch the weapon sail through the room. A fist connects with my jaw, and the contact sends me to the ground and into broken glass. The pain has me quickly getting back up. Victor is getting to his feet, too. Glass rains down as he shakes off all the broken bottles and glasses. The smell of alcohol is strong, and I grip the bar so I don't slip.

The security man on the ground isn't dead. His leg jerks, but I stay focused on Victor. He takes a look at the gun across the room and starts running to it. I pick up a bucket of ice and let it sail. It hits him on the back of the head. He doesn't fall but stops, holding his head. I'm racing after him as his knees buckle. He kicks out, surprising me, and I hit the ground hard. He moves to get up, and I kick out, connecting with the back of his legs. I stand and grab a vase on the coffee table and bring it down on his head. It buys me time to do what I want. Removing my belt, I wrap it around his throat, just like he must have done to Raven. I allow everything she told me to pour through me, and I use the image of her crying and hurt to give me power. I pull the belt as hard as I can. Victor tries to pull it off, but all the blows to the head have weakened him.

"Now you know how she felt," I tell him as I pull harder, hoping to snap his fucking neck. He fights and tries to rise, but I slam my knee into his spine before tugging on the belt around his neck again. With everything I have, I hold tight as he struggles. I fall to the ground too as he tries to get away, but I hold firm and roll with him, as I refuse to let the belt go, and I don't loosen my hold when Victor stops fighting, not even when he stops moving completely.

A gunshot splits the air, and the bullet misses me by an inch. I look into the eyes of the dying security man who fired his last shot but missed. His eyes are devoid of life now, and I release the belt and take stock of the trashed room and the dead bodies.

The hotel room doors are closed, and I get up but quickly sit back down. The blows I took and the blood that has soaked into my shirt show me that my injuries might be a bit more than a few scratches. I lift up my shirt and see the source of the blood—a cut along my side. It must have happened from all the glass behind the bar. I hold my side as I get up again and make my way to the doors to lock them.

I have no idea what I'm going to do now, but I can't leave. My hand rests on the handle when the door opens. I'm ready to race for the gun when Gilly stops me.

"Well now. You really made a fucking mess." Gilly sounds delighted as he takes in all the dead bodies.

"He hurt Raven," I say and walk slowly into the room. I still need the gun, but turning my back on Gilly feels wrong, and being unarmed feels worse. "What are you doing here?" I ask. Was he reporting back to Victor?

"I got a message from Victor to come."

I frown as Gilly takes out his phone. "When?"

Gilly looks at the message. "About fifteen minutes ago."

When I arrived. Gilly must be his insurance that if I hurt him, I didn't get away with it.

I contemplate shooting Gilly. He is the only witness.

He puts his phone away, and for the first time, he seems to comprehend what he just stepped into.

"You were watching Raven for him?" I ask and my anger resurfaces, but so does the wave of dizziness. I need to rest.

"You don't look so good." There's no concern in Gilly's voice. He's making a call.

"Who are you ringing?" I'm tempted to raise my gun.

"Relax, Aidan. I'm just getting a cleanup crew."

I can't fucking relax. But I listen as Gilly, true to his word, calls for a cleanup crew.

"So, what is your story here?" Gilly asks as he steps around the still security man and stops at Victor's dead body. My belt is still around his neck. I manage to keep the gun in my hand and remove my belt from around Victor's neck.

It's then my phone rings, and I answer it without taking my eyes off Gilly.

"Are you close by?" Jason asks.

"Is Raven okay?" My heart races.

Silence.

I'm walking to the door and open it when Jason replies. "She was snooping in your office."

Why do his words hurt so fucking much? "I'm on my way." I look back at Gilly.

"I'll take care of things here," he says.

I don't trust him, but right now I have no choice.

"Wait," Gilly says as he strips off his suit jacket and walks to me, holding it out.

I take the jacket and slip it on. "Thanks."

"There's more," Jason continues as I get the jacket on and leave the hotel suite.

"What?"

"You need to stay calm."

I'm walking faster. "Tell me."

"She's with Frank."

I forget my pain and I'm running. I have no idea if I'll get there in time.

CHAPTER TWENTY SIX

Raven

I'M IN AIDAN'S ROOM, and all I can do is pace the floor. My nails are chewed to nothing. I have never felt so stupid or screwed. Jason will tell Aidan, and when he does... I can't finish that thought. I could say I was in there to use the phone, but Jason caught me at the safe.

Tears burn my eyes, and when a loud knock draws my attention away from my fretting, I don't feel relief when Lily appears from the half-open door. Her face is drawn as she frowns. She steps into the room and onto the luxurious silvery rug that covers the bedroom floor.

She bobs her head, causing her blonde hair to bounce. "Master Frank requests your presence in the drawing room." She purses her lips.

My heart jumps so fast in my chest that a wash of dizziness has me reaching out to steady myself.

"Why?" I ask, my hands instantly running the length of my black dress. He could just be giving his condolences. I try to calm my frantic thoughts. "Frank, as in Aidan's uncle?" I quiz, hoping she's wrong. I have avoided the man, but Lily gives an almost apologetic smile that screams—*I'm afraid that you heard me correctly.*

"I have no idea why. I was sent to get you."

"Okay." I hold my head high and do what I do best, shake off emotions and remember to stay calm. My mask of indifference settles into place.

Lily hasn't moved from the door, and my unease turns into dread that ticks away like a bomb.

"What is it?" I ask. My heart *thump, thump, thumps.*

"He's not alone." She pivots quickly; her movements remind me of an unbalanced spinning top, but before she tumbles over, she rights herself and progresses across the landing. Being requested by Frank has fear growing and clawing at the wall of my stomach. As Lily proceeds to the staircase that widens toward the bottom and brings us to the ground floor, that sense of terror amplifies.

With control comes a steadiness to my hands and a gentler beat of my heart. I shut off all my emotions as the large wooden double doors leading to the drawing room are pushed open, and I halt briefly as Frank starts to rise from the chaise lounge in the drawing room.

"Raven, please take a seat." Frank pushes his bloody hands against the seat he has just offered me. The once stunning golden and cream fabric is now soiled.

One step, two steps.

I swallow the bile that advances up my esophagus. I sit down slowly on the opposite side of the chaise lounge. The bolster cushion has survived the bloody mess. My gaze follows the drops of blood, like an Easter egg hunt, until they stop at the man secured to a chair. The source of the blood loss is a large gash on the left-hand side of his torso.

"You will have to wait a moment, Raven." Frank flashes a smile while picking up a knife from the nest of mahogany tables. The white strip of fabric in the man's mouth does nothing to muffle the screams that spill from his lips.

I pick a spot on the wall. Green wallpaper with small purple roses becomes my sole focus. Tears fall as the man's wails puncture a hole in my façade. My heart thuds as the shrieks flood the room. I whimper. I've never felt this level of helplessness. I'm sitting here while a man fights for his life. When his screams finally stop, I wipe falling tears off my cheeks.

"Now, where was I?" Frank's voice has me glancing at him. He holds the knife tightly in his hand.

I swallow. *Is this my end? Will everything I have done up to this point been in vain?* The fear I tried to keep at bay is uncontrollably wild as Frank strides toward me with a smile that makes my heart jackhammer.

"I know a lot about you, Raven." Frank takes a white handkerchief from his shirt pocket and uses it to clean the blood from the knife. "Like, I know you stole from Victor."

I shake my head.

He stops wiping down his knife and waggles a finger at me. "Don't lie. You lie, and that will make me angry."

I swallow the bile and stay as still as a stone.

Frank takes my silence for compliance and continues cleaning his knife. "I know your father is bankrupt."

Everything inside me sinks down into my shoes. It's over.

"I know that Jason caught you trying to steal from Aidan." Frank has reached me and kneels down so we're eye to eye.

Fear twists every organ painfully until I think I'm going to snap. Tears are forced from my eyes, and Frank smiles and watches them drip off my chin.

"I mean, I made it easy leaving the safe open. Just like I left your bedroom door open and even kept maids and security away." He grins before reaching out and wiping a tear off my cheek with his thumb. My chest tightens when he licks my tear from his finger. "It was exhausting, and all the while you stayed in your room."

My body pulses, but I don't feel my feet on the floor or my hands on the cushions. Even his words are dreamlike, and I wonder if I am about to pass out. Is this what leaving your body feels like?

"I also know what my son did to you."

I jerk back at his words as my vision wavers.

"That won't happen again." Frank rises and steps away from me.

I suck in sharp gulps of air before looking at the double doors. I need to run. There's nothing keeping me here. This is a mess. They know everything. The thought of losing Aidan has tears streaming down my face.

"You have gotten too close to Aidan. You need to leave." Frank turns back to me. I'm not sure if I heard him right. The door opens, and a man enters carrying a large black bag.

He drops it close to Frank's leg before leaving.

"You can take this money and leave."

I'm confused. "You're letting me go?"

Frank nods. "Yes."

I'm not stupid. I can't just walk away from what I've done. Frank sees my hesitation.

"Killing you would only have Aidan in a frenzy, looking for your killer. So, if you leave now, I won't tell him the truth about you. Just stay away and I'll take care of the rest."

I want to ask if I'm that big of a threat. Frank brings the bag over to me and settles it at my feet before opening it. It's stacked high with hundred-euro notes. I take out a bundle. There must be hundreds of thousands here. This would give me and Louise a new start.

I glance back up at Frank.

"I won't lie. I wish I could kill you," he grits out but jumps back as the double doors open.

My pulse hits a peak that sends my head rushing as Aidan steps in, and he doesn't look good. His gaze takes in the room: the money in my hand, the bag at my feet,

Frank still brandishing a knife, and the man who's dead on the chair, before his gaze settles on me again.

I drop the money and get up. "What happened?" I walk to him on unsteady legs and reach out, but he pulls away, not allowing me to touch his face. The rejection hurts.

"Raven was just leaving," Frank says.

I glance at Frank as he puts the knife away and picks up the bag of money. My heart slams into my chest as he walks to me and holds out the bag. "Safe travels," he says.

"She doesn't want your money." Aidan's words are heavy, and the closer I look at him, the better I see cuts along his neck and one close to his hairline. He looks like he's been in a brawl.

"I beg to differ." Frank grins.

Aidan steps forward. "Raven is going nowhere. So you can put your money away."

Frank's face twists with anger. "I'm trying to protect you, son."

I'm looking at the bag of money. Could I grab it and run? Would Frank hold Aidan back? My throat tightens.

"Jason caught her in your office," Frank says.

The world spins and I can't even look at Aidan. He'll surely kill me.

"I know."

My head snaps toward Aidan. He knows?

"You know?" Frank repeats what I'm thinking. For the first time, he really takes in Aidan's appearance. "Where were you?"

Aidan's face grows paler, and he looks ready to fall, yet he stays upright. "I was killing Victor."

My heart jumps and I reach out again for Aidan, but his glare cuts me deeper than any knife possibly could.

Frank doesn't respond straight away, and when he does, it's with a roar that pulls the soul from my body. He lurches forward and hits Aidan in the face with a closed fist.

Watching Aidan fall to the ground catches on something primal, and I'm standing over him squaring up to Frank. "Don't touch him," I shout.

Frank's face twists in rage, but I stand my ground. Something behind me catches his attention. I don't look over my shoulder, even though I want to. I won't leave Aidan unprotected. I take a peek at the unconscious giant at my feet.

"He killed Victor," Frank snarls.

Movement along my side has my whole body tightening with anticipation. Waiting feels almost worse than death itself.

Jason walks past me and steps into the room. His face is a picture of calm, yet his stormy eyes tell me there is a war brewing, and it appears to be with me. I tighten my fists, not in strength but to stop my fingers from trembling. I am no match for these men. The fact they haven't killed me gives me a sliver of bravery.

"Gilly is with the cleanup crew." Jason runs a hand along his chin while tilting his head. He's assessing me like I'm a problem. Clearly I am.

"At least someone is acting appropriately," Frank settles on. "I'm surprised it's my son." He exhales, but his gaze fires up when it lands on me before it drips like molten lava onto Aidan.

"Let me get him cleaned up." Jason walks toward his brother. It's only then that I see a flash of fear in his eyes, but it's gone quickly.

"He doesn't deserve to live," Frank says.

Jason nods, and I feel the betrayal for Aidan.

"He's useful, and I'm sure the Bratva knew this might happen." Jason fires me a look that has me hunching my shoulders.

"If they want him dead, then that's what I will be forced to do." Frank steps closer to Jason.

There's a long pause, and I'm waiting for Jason to fight for his brother, but instead he nods. "We all know the risks. I'm sure Aidan knew that when he set off on this crusade."

I flinch when Jason's gaze lands on me. "I'm still struggling to understand why." Disgust fills Jason's features, and my face burns. "Step aside."

As much as I want to run, I don't move away from Aidan. I don't trust Jason. He hasn't exactly stuck up for Aidan. When I don't move straight away, Jason steps closer.

"Now, Raven." His voice is so low, but I see a flash of fear again in his eyes, and that's what makes me move. He heaves his brother off the ground.

"You should take the money while you can." Frank speaks behind me as Jason manages to drag Aidan to the door.

Jason stops. "He's right. You should leave." Jason pulls an unconscious Aidan from the room, and I'm left with Frank, who unties the man from the chair. His body hits the ground with a thud. I jump and swallow.

The bag of money is right in front of me. Tears blur my vision, and with clenched fists, I walk out of the room and rush after Jason. He hasn't gotten far; in fact, he's halfway down the hallway. I run to him and slide my frame under Aidan's other arm. Tossing his arm around my shoulder, I grip his waist and take as much of his weight as I can. Jason doesn't say anything as we carry Aidan to a guest room.

"Lower him as slowly as you can," Jason instructs.

I'm sweating and finding it hard to breathe fully while I do as Jason says. Aidan is sprawled out on the bed. His suit jacket has parted, and the bloody shirt gives me pause.

"Get Doctor Riley here." Jason speaks into his phone before he sits at his brother's bedside. "Aidan, you have got to wake up." He slaps him on the cheek, but Aidan doesn't react.

I'm frozen watching the bloody patch soak all the white out of the shirt. Jason starts to open the shirt, and I see the large gash on Aidan's torso.

"Fuck." Jason's gaze sparks with anger as he glares at me. "Get me some towels," he grits while pointing at a door behind me.

I rush into the bathroom and grab a stack of towels. I throw one at Jason. He catches it and presses the white fabric to Aidan's side.

Aidan groans, and his eyes flicker open. He's staring at his brother.

"What did you do?" Jason barks.

I want to tell Jason to leave him alone, but I keep my mouth shut.

"I told you not to kill him." Jason shakes his head.

"He didn't deserve to live," Aidan mumbles. He licks his wet lips. "Raven?"

Jason exhales in annoyance. I lean in and try to take Aidan's hand. His head snaps to me, and he pulls his hand away from my touch. Once again, his rejection hurts.

"I'm sorry." I am. I'm so sorry he got hurt.

"He needs to rest," Jason grits out.

I try not to cry as I nod.

Aidan is still looking at me, and I wish he would do his worst to me so he would stop looking at me with such anger in his eyes.

The door opens, and who I can assume is the doctor enters. He opens his bag, and Jason steps aside to let the doctor work.

"I'll be outside with Raven," Jason informs Aidan.

I don't want to go anywhere with Jason, but I follow him out the door. The minute we're in the hallway, Jason turns his back on me. He hates me.

"I had no choice."

Jason fires a narrowed glance at me over his shoulder. "I don't care."

"I do. I care for Aidan."

He snorts. "You care about money."

My hands tighten into fists, and I step up to Jason. "If I cared about money, I would have taken the bag that Frank offered me and left." If I had a lick of sense, I would have left.

My stomach squirms. I promised Louise I would get her out of there, and the one shot I had, I blew. This time, I walk away from Jason as the reality of what I have done comes crashing down around my shoulders. The weight has me kneeling down like I might get better air quality down here.

"Why did you stay?" Jason asks. "You know this won't end well. For you or for my brother." Pain sparks to life, and Jason shakes his head, his features tight.

"I love him," I admit out loud for the first time.

"Do you think love is going to stop the Bratva from ripping you both to shreds?" He's towering over me, and I grip the wall to help me stand. Jason is terrifying, and I have another moment of regretting my decision to stay.

"I don't know," I half cry. "I'm so sick..." I shake my head. "Victor deserved to die."

"That's great, Raven. Maybe he did. But since my brother met you, every decision he has made has been reckless." Jason points at the door, then runs his hand down his face. "My brother disobeyed our leader. You have no idea of what he has done for you."

"I do. I know exactly what he did for me. That's why I'm not going home to take my sister away from our abusive father. That's why I'm standing here in a hallway with you." Tears fall, heavy with anger and the truth that I have picked Aidan over my sister.

I pray to God she can forgive me.

"You can still leave," Jason says, not getting what I'm saying.

I lose any semblance of self-preservation. Maybe it's everything I have suffered. Maybe it's being so close to the edge that finally pushes me over.

"I didn't leave when you caught me in the office. I didn't leave when Frank offered me money." I take a step up to Jason. "I didn't leave when Gilly forced himself on me." I'm screaming. I'm losing the will to stay calm. I'm falling so hard off the cliff of sanity that I don't notice the door opening.

The first thing I register is the horror on Jason's face before I turn and face the open doorway, where Aidan stands with fury flaming in his eyes.

CHAPTER TWENTY SEVEN

Aidan

JASON IS THE SECOND eldest, yet my whole life I've thought of him as the eldest. I've looked up to my brother. I've listened to him. But as he places a hand on my shoulder and draws me away from Raven, I'm two seconds away from shaking him off.

Raven said Gilly abused her. All I can think is I've let her down. The abuse must have happened under my roof.

I had just gotten a text from Gilly saying he was on his way here. He must have wanted to talk about where we go from here. That's what made me get up off the bed, what made me go to the door to let Jason know. I didn't think in a million years I would hear all her confessions, especially the last one, that Gilly had forced himself on her.

"Gilly is Frank's son. The next to rule." Jason's voice is low, like he can dip under my wall of anger and reach the sensible part of me.

I shrug him off. All I am is anger, that is, until I face Raven and take in the devastated look on her face.

"Please, Aidan..." She's shaking her head as tears fall from her eyes.

"You need to rest." The doctor speaks behind me. I see nothing else but Raven.

I take a controlled step toward her. I've never wanted to take the pain from someone so much. I would use up my time here on this earth to right the wrongs done to her.

I think of this girl protecting her sister. I think of her underneath me as we made love. I think of her strength when her mother died. I think of strength to hide something of this caliber from me. I want to ask why she didn't tell me. Instead, I take her face in my hands. Her whimper wobbles, and she closes her eyes. Tears of pain wet my palm.

"Look at me, Raven."

She does. Her eyelashes are dark and heavy from all the tears she has spilt.

"I love you," I admit.

She takes in a sharp breath.

Jason shifts behind me.

None of this matters. I love her and everything she has done wasn't out of greed. I don't know the full story, but I'm sure after this is all over, she will tell me.

"I'm going to take you somewhere safe," I promise her before I lean in and press my lips against hers. I taste her pain, and when she responds to my kiss, I use all my willpower to pull my lips from hers and release her.

I don't speak as I step around Raven.

"What are you doing?" Jason shouts after me. I'm barely walking, but adrenaline and the want for blood drives me down the hallway. My shirt flaps on either side of me, and I stop in the hallway, retrieving a gun from its secret place under the table.

Jason is behind me. I'm waiting for him to stop me, but instead, he's on the phone. "Get everyone here," he says before hanging up. I have no idea who he called, and frankly, I don't care.

"You need to rethink this," Jason tries to reason with my madness.

"You don't even know what I'm thinking." I check the chamber of the gun. It's loaded.

Jason blocks me. "I know you want to kill Gilly."

I nod. "That's what I'm going to do."

Jason's jaw tightens. "You kill him and Frank will kill you."

I can't look at Jason. I won't allow him to talk me out of this.

"Aidan, Raven won't survive without you. What will Frank do after he kills you?"

I swallow the fear that claws at me. "He hurt Raven under my roof, Jason. She's to be my wife. I have every right to retaliate."

"Are you really conspiring to kill my son?" Frank asks as he steps into the hallway. He appears relaxed. Calm. Like he doesn't have a care in the world. Like I'm not a threat. I suppose he has the right to feel like that when he rules over us. But, I've never felt this way about anyone, so I don't give two shits who he rules over.

Jason spins, and his hand goes to the band of his trousers. He doesn't remove his weapon, though. It's a reflex. He thinks quickly and makes the action appear as if he was fixing his jacket. Maybe I read the signals wrong.

"Aidan is upset," Jason starts.

Frank sneers. "He seems to be very temperamental lately." He hates me, but not as much as I hate him.

"Gilbert harmed Raven." Jason speaks in my defense. I don't give a rat's ass about explaining myself to Frank. All I want is to be ready for when Gilly walks through my door to beam about cleaning up my mess and then I can pull the fucking trigger. From the relaxed pose of Frank, he has no idea that his son is on the way.

"That is a very unfortunate matter." I'm not shocked at Frank's response. He knew what his son did.

"You want someone like him leading?" I sneer.

"Aidan." Raven's soft voice behind me has me turning.

"Go back," I say to her.

Her gaze darts to the gun in my hand. "Please, don't do this." Raven glances at Frank and Jason before running her hands down the side of her dress. "You need to rest." Her eyes widen, like she's pleading with me to follow her back to the bed. I'm tempted. I really am.

The front door opens, and I see who Jason rang; Alex, William, and even Matty arrive.

"What is this?" Frank smiles, but he doesn't seem so sure of himself.

When my brothers cross the threshold, one other person follows behind.

Gilly.

I'm walking toward him.

He notices the gun in my hand and reaches for his own. Everything happens so quickly.

"Don't fucking move." The cock of the gun behind me has me freezing as Frank issues his threat.

My gun is already raised and trained on Gilly. He's withdrawn his own gun, and it's also pointed at my head. More guns are withdrawn.

"Go back," Jason orders, and I turn slightly to see Raven running down the hall and out of the line of fire. All of my brothers have guns trained on Frank.

"You pull that trigger, and I'll pull mine," Frank snarls.

"I just cleaned up your fucking mess!" Gilly shouts with a look of pure confusion on his face.

I clench my jaw, and my finger tightens on the trigger. If I shoot, so will Frank, but what about my brothers?

"Drop your weapons," Frank orders my brothers. They have to obey. He is our leader, so when they don't, everything in me swells with pride.

"What is going on?" Gilly asks.

"Shut up," Frank snarls again. "I'll banish him. You will never see him again." I'm surprised at Frank negotiating.

Alex, Matty, and William are in my line of sight. They don't blink or waver from their stance.

"Take the deal," Jason says from behind me.

"It's not enough," I admit.

Gilly's eyes widen.

"You can't take my son's life, Aidan." For the first time, I hear the fear in Frank's voice.

We're in a standoff.

"Think of Raven," Jason throws out, and he's right. If I shoot Gilly, Frank will shoot me and maybe take out one of my brothers too. Where does that leave Raven? Back in the hands of her father.

"If he ever crosses my path again, I will kill him," I grind out, not happy.

"Is this about Raven?" Gilly asks, and he has the balls to appear astonished.

"Everyone needs to lower their guns. We must remember we are family." Frank issues the reminder. I can't lower mine, but I know I drew first, so I need to lower mine first.

"You will never put your hands on her again," I grit out.

He won't hold my gaze, and it takes me another few seconds before I lower my gun.

"Lower yours, Gilbert," Frank orders and Gilly does.

I glance at Frank, and his gun is already lowered. Slowly, my brothers lower their weapons, and we all put them away.

"Get him out of my home," I order Frank as the energy is zapped out of me. From the corner of my eye, I see Raven still watching. She should have gotten to safety.

"Where the fuck am I meant to go?" Gilly grows brave when he doesn't have a gun pointed at his head.

"You will stay with your mother." Frank walks past me and to his son. "Come on." He's in a hurry to get Gilly out of my home. I know I have to pay the price for my actions today, but eliminating Victor was worth it.

"No. Dad, I'm next to rule. I can't hide away. The Bratva won't be happy."

I watch as Frank grips Gilly's arm. "You put your hands on his girl. Did you think you could get away with it? Now come on."

Alex walks toward me with a look of relief on his face.

I meet Gilly's eyes, and he's infuriated at being banished. I grin to rub salt in the wound, as that's all the power I have right now.

"Fuck him!" Gilly shouts. "She loved it."

I don't know what Frank sees on my face, but he shifts his body in front of his son.

"Don't!" Jason roars as I aim the gun at Gilly.

There's a tenth of a second when his eyes widen, and I pull the trigger. Blood from the head wound splatters across Frank, who's already spinning with his own gun drawn on me. I don't get to fire my gun a second time as Frank squeezes his trigger.

I'm falling as someone tackles me from the side, but not before my face blazes with pain. Another bullet is fired and hits Frank in the shoulder, sending him sailing back. Jason dives to the floor as Frank returns fire. William and Matty are on the ground taking cover. I blink through the pain to see Frank scramble out the open front door. Matty and William get off the ground and race out the door after Frank. Alex gets off me, and I reach up and touch my face. The bullet grazed my cheek.

The noise of running feet has us all turning as Raven rushes past my brothers and kneels at my feet. "Oh, God, Oh God." She's touching my face, and I bite the hiss.

"I thought... I thought he shot you." She's running her hands down my chest and skips over the bandaged wound on my side. Her hands shake uncontrollably. Raven takes Jason's outstretched hand to help her up. She accepts it with hesitation. Alex gets up off the ground.

"I'm okay," I say to Raven.

She's shaking her head. "No, you're not."

"I'll be fine, Raven." I nod, and she nods with me, but I can see the disbelief clear in her eyes. I think she's in shock.

Jason reaches down his hand and pulls me off the ground. Raven stands beside me, and I don't release my brother's hand.

"You shot Frank," I say. Jason looks troubled. I don't blame him. That shouldn't have happened. "We can say I'm the one who shot Frank."

"Right now, you need to lie down," Jason responds.

Alex nods in agreement. "I'll go help find Frank. He's still alive." Alex leaves, and I can't let Jason's hand go. "Thank you." I can't express what he did for me.

He seems uncomfortable with the praise. "Don't mention it."

I snort. "All of Ireland will be mentioning it."

Shooting a leader isn't something that will be brushed under the carpet.

We're fucked.

I release Jason's hand and turn to Raven.

Was it worth it? Yes, for Raven it was. What this all means for my family? I have no idea.

CHAPTER TWENTY EIGHT

Raven

"ARE YOU SURE?" I'M holding a file in my hand. I know it's only paper, but what's on that paper is life changing. I glance up into eyes that burn.

"This is what your father wanted. So, you give it to him." Aidan touches my cheek.

He has done so much for me, and this gesture has my fingers tightening on the paper. Giving my father the information so he can buy property cheap will give me access to Louise and my freedom.

But the cost to Aidan is millions.

He killed Victor. He killed Gilly. He's slowly killing me with his love.

My stomach quivers. "Aidan, you can't just hand me all this." I wave the file. He knows what I'm saying. Frank is missing. It's been days since the shootout in Aidan's home, but he still rules over them.

Aidan moves forward, and with a smile on his face, he leans in. "I would burn down a city for one kiss from you." His gaze darts to my mouth.

My pulse pounds along my neck. Butterflies erupt and swirl in my stomach. "Calm down, fire starter. You can kiss me."

His laughter dances across my face, and I grow weak at the knees. When his lips touch mine, I sink into Aidan. The truth is, he would burn a city to the ground. But the fear that we might be standing in the city while he incinerates it grips me.

Killing Victor and Gilly won't go unnoticed, and the uncertain future we have makes me uneasy every day.

Aidan breaks the kiss. "Let's go get your sister."

Joy, excitement, and elation have me beaming up at Aidan. "Let's go get my sister." I repeat his words as we leave the house and get into the car.

The country house we're staying in is smaller than Aidan's home, but its charm alone has won me over. This is where we will bring Louise, too. Someplace she can be safe. Someplace I can take care of her.

I'm equal parts happy and nervous. Aidan reaches out and takes my hand. I'm still gripping the file on my lap in the car. I want to ask him again if he's sure about this. When I glance at him, he raises both brows. "I'd prefer to kill your father, so this is the second option: to do it peacefully."

I swallow and finally accept that I'm giving my father the information he requested. The days after Gilly's death, I told Aidan everything. He listened to me with patience. I could see the disappointment in his eyes when he asked me why I didn't come to him for help. I suppose I was so used to people disappointing me that I didn't really think Aidan would help me.

I was very wrong.

We pull up to my father's house. I called ahead and told him we would be arriving. The gates open as the car pauses outside.

"I will be with you the entire time," Aidan reminds me.

I want to laugh. I haven't had one second on my own. Aidan hasn't left my side since he found out about Gilly, so the idea of him not being with me seems ridiculous.

I leave the file on my lap and squeeze his leg. The action is simple, but he stiffens and my mind goes south, my core tightening.

"Thank you." I remove my hand.

He nods.

"I don't think I can ever repay you." I'm frowning, searching for the right words, which are currently failing me.

The car stops, and Aidan unbuckles his seat belt.

"You can repay me. I've already thought of several ways." He's serious.

My stomach squeezes. Would I be working for the Mafia? I nod in agreement. I would pay this enormous debt back.

Aidan reaches out and unbuckles my belt. "I'm going to accept sexual favors as payments."

A laugh whistles past my lips. "Aidan, be serious." I shove his shoulder with little force. I'm still aware of his wounds. The one on his cheek looks tender.

He smiles. "I'm deadly serious. I mean, I want all of you every night."

I smile into his smile.

"I want kisses on demand." He takes a kiss, and my heart soars with how he looks at me.

"I love you," I tell him like it's the first time, but it feels more like the hundredth time.

His smile softens along the edges. "I love you, too."

He leans his forehead against mine before he presses another kiss to my lips. "I'm serious about the kisses."

I wrestle with a smile. "Okay."

He gives a featherlight kiss before he leans away. I grip the file and wait as Aidan gets out of the car and walks around the front with so much swagger that my knees would buckle if I weren't sitting down. When he opens my door and holds out his hand, I inhale a long breath and let myself know I can do this.

I'm not alone.

I have Aidan.

***

"I think Daisy should be her name." Louise strokes the white bunny that Aidan gave me. We sit out on the back lawn of what will be our home.

"I really like Bob," I declare, picking up my book, Northanger Abbey by Jane Austen, which I've been trying to read for the last hour, only to be interrupted by Louise every two seconds. But I actually don't mind her interruptions.

Louise tucks the bunny close to her chest as she leans against the large oak tree. "Bob? It's a girl." She rolls her eyes, and the dramatic action makes me smile. There's no fear in her eyes, no haunted look that greeted me only two days ago when I went with Aidan to give my father the information he had requested and collect my sister. All that is gone. Her gaze smiles at me.

I tuck my book under my arm before I reach out and take her hand. "We will call her Daisy," I agree. I have no idea how to express what I'm feeling. But when Louise threads her fingers through mine and holds on tight, I know she must be feeling as overwhelmed as I am.

We're finally free.

My father kept to his word. I honestly think it was only because Aidan was with us. Otherwise, I'm sure he wouldn't have taken the file and handed Louise over so easily.

I got to say goodbye to Betty, the house manager. I always favored her over everyone else. Betty is a different kind of breed. She always inspired me to be stronger. I think I've finally found my strength.

I tighten my hold on Louise's small hand before letting it go.

The cloudless blue sky above our heads has me lying back with my novel tucked securely to my chest.

"What are you girls doing?" Aidan's voice has me rolling from my back and onto my stomach. His tone matches his appearance. He's smiling down at me. The yellow T-shirt looks good on him, as does the guitar strung across his back. I'm kneeling up as he sits down beside Louise and me.

"I'm taking care of Daisy while Raven ignores us," Louise declares with a smile on her face. Seeing my sister so happy and safe has everything in me settling. Like dust on old bones.

"Can you blame me?" I wave my book in his face.

"Please, by all means, continue to read while I..." Aidan takes the guitar off his back. "Sing a song for Louise."

"Ohhhh." Louise waggles her brows and shimmies her shoulders like she's settling in for a show. And she is. Watching Aidan play the guitar and sing sends me into a trance. He's that good.

He strums out a few notes and winks at me. My heart soars, and my book is forgotten as he belts out The Calling's "Wherever You Will Go."

When Aidan finishes playing, Louise raises her hand to her forehead and pretends to swoon. The smile on Aidan's face has me wanting to reach out, take his hand, and drag him upstairs. But instead of acting on my desires, I sit back and smile at him, the man I love, before I look at my sister as she continues to stroke Daisy.

We once were victims of victims.

But victims heal.

I've healed.

CHAPTER TWENTY NINE

AIDAN

THREE WEEKS OF TORTURE, waiting, praying, hiding away from what we know we must face. And we will face our fates today. The Bratva has finally reached out. They want Jason, Alex, and me to attend a meeting that they've decided will take place in my home. I'm surprised they would allow us to meet them on our own turf.

I slip on my beige suede jacket with the fur collar. It wasn't always my favorite but a gift from my father. I find it a fitting garment to wear today.

"I don't want you to go." Raven chews on her lip as she stands in the doorway of our bedroom. Life here with her and Louise has been perfect. I meet Raven's striking gaze in the mirror. Looking at her still steals away a piece of my darkness every time.

Today, I need my darkness. Today, I need my anger. I need to wear my violence like a badge if I am to survive.

I turn to Raven. "I have to. I won't be long."

She looks away from me. “You don’t know that.” Fear strangles her words, cutting them short.

“I do. I will make it back to you, Raven.” One way or another. I just hope it’s not in a box. I pull her into my arms, and she grabs my waist. Her fists tighten in my shirt.

“I have no regrets. I’d kill both of them all over again.” I press a kiss to the crown of her head.

“It won’t be worth it if I lose you.” Her nightmare pours over my shirt, the warm liquid dampening my chest.

I make her look at me. “You will never lose me. I’m yours.”

She’s smiling through her fear, and fuck me, this is why I love her. “You need to promise me you will remain here with Louise.”

She’s nodding. “I’ll wait for you.”

I can’t stop the smile that twists my lips as I press a kiss on her forehead. I have more security around the house than what is necessary. But, with Frank on the loose and no doubt gunning for my head along with the Bratva, I need to keep Raven safe.

“Where is Louise?” I ask to distract Raven.

She sniffles. “She’s with Daisy.”

“I’m beginning to think she’s claimed him as her pet.”

Raven smiles, and I use the moment to take her hand and leave the room. “Daisy’s a girl.” Raven dips her head. Her eyes tell me she knows what I’m doing. The minute we reach the ground floor, I call out to Louise.

Raven will do anything to keep her sister safe, and she knows I need to go in order to stop anyone from harming them.

Louise appears with Daisy tightly held against her chest. "Do you not worry it will poo on you?" I ask.

Louise pulls a face and covers the bunny's ears. "Don't say such a thing. Daisy doesn't poo."

Raven's watching me, chewing her lip, and my gut tightens.

"I'm going out for a few hours. Take care of Raven for me?" I ask Louise. There's a shift in her stance. I think she understands that I'm not going out to pick up groceries.

She nods somberly. "I will."

I'm ready to turn to Raven when Louise and Daisy press themselves against my chest. I slowly wrap my arms around Louise. "Be careful," she whispers.

Raven's eyes are wide with panic and before she can think too much, I release Louise. I don't allow Raven a moment to speak, kissing her like I've never kissed her before. I kiss her like it's our first kiss, I kiss her like it's our last, and I kiss her like I can take all her fears away.

"I love you," I say before releasing her. If I don't go now, I never will.

"I love you, too." Her voice follows me out the door with so much fucking emotion that I almost falter. As I get into the car, I remind myself that I have no choice. I can't hide from Frank, and I most certainly can't hide from the Bratva.

***

My home—my father's home—is like a training base for the Bratva. They seem to be everywhere, unpacking equipment from vans and carrying them inside. I push the pedal to the floor and jam on the brake at the front door. The screech has some of the men looking, but they dismiss me quickly.

Alex is standing at the front door, his hands dug deeply in his pockets, his face a mask of indifference, but this shit right here has got to be killing him. This is our family's home. Forcing myself to stay as calm as possible, I get out of the car.

Alex doesn't speak as I climb the steps to the front door. Once we're shoulder to shoulder, only then does he speak. "They've taken over the house."

"I can see that." I scan the front as they continue to carry steel suitcases and crates into the house. Is this one of Frank's orders to really hurt us? If it is, he's accomplished what he set out to achieve.

"Is Jason here?" I ask, pivoting and crossing the threshold into my home. The first thing I'm drawn to is the bullet hole in the wall from when Frank shot at me.

Bastard.

"He's with the negotiator."

My footfalls pause. Alex grips my shoulder. "I know," is all my brother says.

There are different ranks in the Bratva. Some men are feared, others are ghosts, and some are so elusive that you never want to meet them in any way.

The negotiator is one of them. He doesn't really negotiate. He's the dividing line between life and death. His terms are final. Dread pulls at my legs, but I force myself to walk. The drawing room doors are open, and it's there I find Jason standing at the fireplace and the negotiator is seated. The chair he sits on isn't one of mine. It's like a throne, and he's propped up on it. His fingers curl around a cane. He's too young for one. A scar from the corner of his brow drags down to the edge of his mouth.

I glance back at Jason. His gaze softens as he takes in my coat. I give my brother a slight smile.

"Aidan Murphy, welcome. Alex Murphy, welcome back." The negotiator speaks, and we face him like we're men on trial. We aren't really on trial, as our fates have already been decided.

He doesn't say Jason's name, and I glance at my brother, but he raises his hand before dropping it. "I've already heard my terms."

I look at the negotiator. "I want to hear his terms."

The negotiator grins. His hand curls around the silver head of his cane. "Very well." His Russian accent isn't very thick, which tells me he's lived here in Ireland for a long time.

I'm not ready to hear what we must face, but I stand still. This is my country, and these are my rules.

"But first we will continue with Alex Murphy."

I want to ask why both my brothers are being punished for my doing, but I remind myself that this isn't really a negotiation. I've never heard of the negotiator bringing terms to The Brigadier to pass on to the higher ranking of the Bratva.

Right now, this is as close as we will get to big players, and it's close enough for me. The fact that we've garnered their attention is enough.

"Alex will rule, as Gilbert Murphy is deceased." The negotiator doesn't flinch as he dishes out the terms. "You will answer to the Bratva, and a monthly meeting will take place."

I'm stepping forward, breaking all the rules, but at this stage, I don't think I can make this any worse. "Frank wanted the O'Reagans taken out. We didn't do that. That's what ties us, isn't it? So If we don't want the O'Reagans wiped out, can't we end this?"

The negotiator laughs in my fucking face.

"I've already tried that," Jason says and steps away from the fireplace to stand to my right.

I glance at Alex. His jaw is tight. I want to tell him I'm sorry for landing him in this situation. I will, but not right now. The negotiator turns to me, and this is the moment I'm dreading. Will they demand my life for Victor's?

"Aidan Murphy." He smirks at me, and I know this is going to be worse than I thought. "You are being judged on the murder of Gilbert Murphy, who would have led the Irish Mafia on our behalf."

What the fuck was Frank thinking allowing this level of control? None of this makes sense. I hope I live to find a way out of this fucking mess.

"We are aware that Gilbert was in Victor's suite the night of Victor's murder. He also had a cleanup crew clear up three dead bodies. So, your killing him was a mercy."

What utter bullshit. They're pinning Victor's death on Gilbert.

I grit my teeth.

"So, we find you not guilty." The negotiator rises.

I step forward, and Jason lands his hand heavily on my shoulder, telling me to be silent. But I can't. They would have seen me leave the room. They know I'm with Raven. My blood was at the scene. This makes no sense.

"That's horseshit," I say.

Alex is the one who exhales.

The negotiator stands with the help of his cane. "Which part?"

All of it, I want to say. "Victor," I say.

He nods and walks toward me. When he stops, he places his cane under his arm and slips on a pair of black gloves.

"Gilbert killed Victor, and you killed Gilbert. To us, Aidan, you are a hero. We don't kill heroes. We also don't bite the hand that feeds us."

I hear the warning. I should take this gift, but it feels like a pretty box with a bomb inside.

"What about Frank?" Unless that was part of Jason's terms, which I still hadn't heard.

"Frank will continue to work with us. He's not a concern. He reacted when his son died, but he knows his place." The negotiator has finished putting on his gloves.

"But Jason shot him, so that won't be overlooked."

My heart thrashes in my chest. What will happen to Jason?

"I have to enter into an arranged marriage," Jason says.

That doesn't sound so bad. I'd joke about it, but the negotiator stands in front me, still watching me. I can see it as clear as day in his gaze. He doesn't like me. Maybe he doesn't like being questioned. But here I was expecting the worst, and so far, it looks like I'm the one walking away with not even a slap on the wrist while my brothers pay the price.

"He must also produce an heir," the negotiator reminds Jason.

I glance at my brother, but he turns away from me. Jason with children? Hard to imagine.

"We will be in touch." The negotiator leaves.

I want to exhale, but both Alex and Jason have turned away from me. Yeah, I feel like that prick.

"I thought they would punish me," I finally say. Two men pass the door carrying crates. "Are these fuckers staying?" I bark and walk to the door, closing it.

"Yes. I must stay here too," Alex says.

"You spoke to the negotiator while I wasn't here?"

Jason finally looks at me. "We negotiated with them over the last week."

"What?" Anger tightens my fists. "You did what?"

"They wanted your head," Alex grits out.

"I didn't think the negotiator negotiated." I run my fingers through my hair.

"They have two Murphys by the balls instead of one Murphy head."

I want to apologize, but it won't change anything.

"So you have to rule over us?" Alex nods, and he appears like the weight of the world is on his shoulders. I'm sure it is.

"You have to marry and produce an heir." I can't wrap my head around that part.

"I have to marry one of their people," Jason admits.

That wouldn't just entwine us for now; that would entwine us forever.

"What has Frank done?" My father will be turning in his grave.

"We use our positions wisely," Jason says, and Alex nods.

"We use these terms to our advantage." Jason steps up to me and Alex.

"We are the Murphys, and no one, especially not these fucking Russians, will take us down." He's nodding at us.

"They think they've won, but we are the Trojan horse that will destroy them from the inside out. We are already in," Alex says. He grips my shoulder while Jason grips my other one, and unspoken words flow between us.

We might be tied to the Bratva for now, but we have a strength that they wouldn't understand. We are brothers.

"Deartháir." We whisper the Irish word for brother, one at a time.

The future is uncertain, but as I leave our father's homestead, I mentally promise one day we will have it back, and one day Raven and I will fill it with children who will have no tie to the Bratva.

But I'm alive and she's safe. She can finally make peace with her past, live in the present, and dream for the future.

***

Want to read Jason and Kira's story? Savage Marriage, book two in the Murphy's Mafia Made Men Series.

Pre-order Today!

WARNING

This book is a dark romance. This book contains scenes that may be triggering to some readers and should be read by those only 18 or older.

TRIGGERS:

Suicide

Murder

Rape

Abuse

Alcohol & Drug Abuse

ABOUT THE AUTHOR

When Vi Carter isn't writing dark romance books, you can find her reading her favorite authors, baking, taking photos, or watching Netflix.

Married with three children, Vi divides her time between motherhood and all the other hats she wears as an Author.

Social Media Links for Vi Carter

Website

Newsletter

Facebook Reader Group

Facebook Author Page

Tiktok

Twitter

Instagram

Bookbub

Goodreads

ACKNOWLEDGMENTS

I'm very lucky to have such amazing readers and Beta Readers. I want to thank the following people who worked with me on this book.

Editor: Sherry Schafer
Proofreader: Michele Rolfe
Proofreader: Amanda Cuff
Blurb was written by: Tami Thomason

Beta Readers
Laura Riley
Lucy Korth
Tami Thomason

Printed in the USA
CPSIA information can be obtained
at www.ICGtesting.com
CBHW021217210224
4566CB00021B/27

9 781915 878229